DEVOURED BY

Doms of Destiny, Colorado 4

Chloe Lang

MENAGE EVERLASTING

Siren Publishing, Inc.
www.SirenPublishing.com

A SIREN PUBLISHING BOOK
IMPRINT: Ménage Everlasting

DEVOURED BY DOMS

ISBN: 978-1-62740-745-8

First Printing: February 2014

Cover design by Les Byerley

Printed in the U.S.A.

PUBLISHER
Siren Publishing, Inc.
www.SirenPublishing.com

DEDICATION

I really appreciate Chloe Vale and her incredibly hard work she delivers on all my books.

Thank you, Chloe. This one is for you.

DEVOURED BY DOMS

Doms of Destiny, Colorado 4

CHLOE LANG

Chapter One

7:03 a.m., Friday – two miles outside Destiny, Colorado

Though Erica Coleman wanted to scream, she couldn't.

Anyone in her current situation—inside the trunk of a speeding car—would need to scream, but the gag around her mouth prevented her from yelling for help. She couldn't move because of the ropes around her ankles and wrists. The hood over her head blinded her and was also making it very difficult to breathe.

All she could do was *listen.*

The roar of the engine rumbled in her ears, muting the voices of her two abductors inside the vehicle.

* * * *

5:40 p.m., Friday – Two Black Knights Tower, Destiny, Colorado

Dylan Strange knew the chances of getting Erica back alive were slim. *Very slim.*

No one had realized that she was missing until billionaire Scott Knight, one of the presidents of Two Black Knights, got an e-mail from the kidnappers.

When they'd checked the TBK system, they'd discovered that Erica hadn't keyed in today at all. Not unusual, given her position as executive assistant to the copresidents. Many days, only Scott and his brother saw her, as she worked on sensitive projects for the two men.

The last person who had seen her was Phoebe Blue at the diner a little before seven this morning. Jason had retraced Erica's steps from her car to the restaurant and found her uneaten bagel, her laptop, and a spilled cup of coffee on the sidewalk by The Green Dragon statue in the park.

The evidence pointed to it being over ten hours since she'd been taken, and less than an hour since the ransom note came in.

Fuck.

They were in the main TBK conference room, which Scott had set up as mission control to find her.

Sheriff Jason Wolfe was pacing around the large table. Scott was at another computer working away feverishly to get the ransom demands in place in case they couldn't find Erica before the set time. Erica's two brothers and their fiancée had left to check out her apartment for any clues they might find.

Why had the kidnappers taken so long to give their demands? Likely, they wanted to make sure Erica was out of Destiny and in a secure place. That was how he would've conducted the same kind of operation. Time was the enemy in this type of investigation. The more hours passed the colder the trail.

Fuck.

He stared at the monitor in front of him, praying for anything that might lead to her.

Nothing.

A man thought of just one thing when he looked at a woman like Erica—and he'd been thinking the same during all his time with her at the gun range. Hell, even his nights had been invaded by images of her, disturbing his sleep. Sex was one of the many compartments of his very structured life. Few could endure such an existence, but it had worked for him for a very long time. Find a willing partner. Maybe dinner. Maybe not. A few hours of wild sex. Move on. No regrets. No emotional bullshit.

But his logic was being shoved to the side by his feelings for Erica. Feelings weren't something he knew how to deal with. Not a good thing given the current circumstances. Her life depended on him being his best, and his best was being analytical and detached. But how the hell could he stay detached when all he could think of was her being in danger?

Fuck.

Keeping his cool was his best weapon, always, but he was having a difficult time doing that at the moment. He adjusted his sunglasses, though they needed no adjusting. Everyone in town knew he wore them indoors and outdoors. What they didn't know was the reason. They were his shield, his armor, his camo. Without his sunglasses, a chance glance from someone—anyone—might reveal his secrets. The risk was too great.

He was the head of security at Two Black Knights Enterprises. This shouldn't have happened on his watch. If the people who had taken Erica harmed a single hair on her pretty head, he would crush them until they were nothing but little tiny piles of shit.

Several computers were on the table. They'd been working on finding her since the ransom e-mail had popped into Scott's inbox just under an hour ago. Whoever was behind this had devised an intricate way for the monies to be sent.

Five international stock exchanges—India, Russia, South Africa, Dubai, and Germany—were part of the scheme. Each had one new company offering stock for purchase. An initial public offering, IPO. Doubtful if any of the companies were legit. Likely they were only fronts. Whatever stock the monies bought would certainly be worthless. The cash would be drained away in microseconds before the local governments had a chance to track it.

A brilliant plan, damn it.

The ransom demanded their stock be purchased at a certain time, ten million each for a grand total of fifty million US dollars.

"How's it coming?" Jason asked Scott.

"The NSE transaction for India is ready to go," the billionaire answered. Everyone in town knew that Scott and his brother thought of Erica as a sister. It was clear he felt guilty for not coming into the office until late afternoon. Scott had told them that he'd wondered why Erica wasn't at her desk at first, but given all she'd been struggling with, he'd dismissed it. Then he'd gotten the e-mail that changed everything. "All I have left to set up is Frankfurt, and then we'll have everything in place."

"Hopefully, we'll find her before you have to do that." The sheriff turned to Dylan. "We don't have much time before Scott has to send the funds for the first purchase."

Dylan didn't look up from the screen. He had to stay focused. "Sheriff, please call out the time every fifteen minutes for me."

"Got it." Jason glanced at the watch on his wrist. "It's five forty-five right now."

Dylan's mind immediately returned to Erica. He'd thought about asking Erica out. He hadn't. Why? Because he couldn't seem to figure out which one of his mental compartments she would fit in. She was a mystery to him. He was certain *moving on* after her would be beyond difficult. Now, there would be no after. No date. Nothing.

At the very least, I should have told Erica how beautiful she is.

So much for the former agent of the CIA keeping his mind on the task at hand.

Damn it, I've got to keep my head clear.

* * * *

8:07 a.m., Friday – an hour from Destiny, Colorado

Being claustrophobic had always been a burden to Erica. In the trunk of her two abductors' car all this time, it was horrific. She wasn't sure what they wanted with her, but a long list of terrible possibilities kept running through her mind.

She'd dreamed of having her own family. Kids. Loving husbands. Recently, she'd been picturing Dylan and Cameron Strange walking her down the aisle one day, though neither had actually seemed to see her as anything other than an executive secretary. It was only a foolish dream—a dream that would not survive the nightmare she was in right now. This wasn't Destiny. This was hell.

Her gun range training with Dylan had helped her get a backbone and relieved some of her ever-present guilt.

Still, another dreadful shiver went up and down her spine.

Though petrified, she tried to remain calm. She wasn't, of course.

Breathe deep.

* * * *

5:56 p.m., Friday – TBK Tower, Destiny, Colorado

Dylan continued moving his fingers over the keyboard at lightning speed. He would've been happier to be out on the scent instead of here, but *here* was where he had to be. Once he found whoever kidnapped Erica, he would get in the field and put a bullet right between their eyes.

"What's 'VU' mean?" Jason asked.

"It's the country code for Vanuatu," he answered.

Though his job in the CIA was mainly acting as an operative, his training in tracking down cyber criminals was extensive. Right now, he was working to ID where Erica's ransom note had originated. He hoped his skills would be enough to rescue her.

"Never heard of Vanuatu before in my whole life." Jason took a seat in one of the leather chairs around the table.

"Most hackers know Vanuatu quite well, especially the big players." Dylan didn't like what he was uncovering. An international crime syndicate had to be behind this. The more he found, the more his hopes for Erica diminished. But he wasn't about to give up. That just wasn't something he could do. Ever. "There are satellite uplinks on Vanuatu. It's a tiny island nation that makes it hard to trace Internet traffic."

Scott moved and sat down beside him again. "That's the fifth country you've mentioned. God, I wish my brother and the Texans were here already."

"When do they get in?" Jason asked.

Scott looked at his iPad. The worry on the man's face mirrored his own. "They just landed. Another hour until they get to Destiny. We could sure use their help right now. Their talents for this kind of thing are incredible."

"I agree," Dylan confessed. "Trust me, Scott. We will find her." *We have to.*

"Yes, we will," Jason said firmly.

"Another dead end." *Damn, whoever sent the ransom note knew how to cover their digital tracks.* "This time Sweden."

"Six o'clock." Jason's time check filled him with trepidation.

"All the transactions are ready to go," Scott announced. "It's five thirty in the morning in India. Their market opens at nine."

India would get the first ten million at 9:30 p.m. local time. Two hours later, Russia, and then thirty minutes after that would be Dubai. Ten million each. The last to go at 1:00 a.m. was South Africa and Germany. Each would receive the last of the fifty million dollars.

Dylan clenched his jaw as he continued his search through the digital muck.

If all the money went to those markets before they got to Erica, there would be no reason for the kidnappers to keep her alive.

* * * *

10:00 a.m., Friday – three hours from Destiny, Colorado

Erica was so antsy being tied up in the trunk. Her mind was racing faster than her heart.

She recalled how Megan, her bosses' fiancée, and Gretchen, the Knights' longtime maid and confidant, had acted during that scary day back on the top floor of TBK Tower. She loved working there with Eric and Scott. At least, she had loved it until a few months ago. Every time since, when she walked into her office, her mind replayed the events of that horrific day.

Eric and Scott were more than bosses to her. Being the youngest and only female of the Orphans of September 28, 2001 in Destiny, Colorado—another tragic day in her life—had bonded her to them. Along with her brothers, Sawyer and Reed, it was like adding an additional five more brothers—Eric and Scott Knight, and Emmett, Bryant, and Cody Stone.

Suddenly, she heard sirens, which pulled her out of her thoughts and back to the here and now—a place she wanted to escape with all her heart.

The car began to slow.

Had the police pulled them over?

Hope sprang up like a fountain.

Her heart thudded even faster in her chest.

She couldn't scream, but she must make noise.

How?

They'd tied her up so that she couldn't kick or move. All she could do was moan as loud as possible.

Please let them hear me.

* * * *

6:36 p.m. – Friday, city limits, Destiny, Colorado

Cameron Strange drove across Silver Spoon Bridge into Destiny, his hometown. He was cutting his two-week vacation short. Seven days on his solo fishing trip had done the trick. He was ready to get back to work.

It was late. Approaching seven.

With another seven days left of his leave, his schedule was clear the rest of the week. No hearings. No depositions. Nothing. He'd head to his office at TBK in the morning after a good night's sleep.

Hell, I could check my messages now.

His phone was dead.

He pulled into Phase Four's parking lot to hook his cell up to the car charger. He couldn't help but grin, knowing everyone at the company, including his brother Dylan, saw him as a workaholic. He was, of course. Work filled his days. There was no one special in his life, no significant other. Why not work?

There'd been one woman that pulled his thoughts away from his job and got him hard in a split second.

Erica.

God, she was unbelievably sexy. The beautiful woman had suffered so much guilt. He was glad that Dylan was coaching her on self-defense. Before the incident at work, where she and others were held at gunpoint, Erica had always sported the most enchanting smile he'd ever seen. Lately, no smile came from her perfect lips. All he'd seen was a heart-wrenching sadness in her eyes.

His office was on the floor below hers. Being the copresidents' personal assistant, Erica's desk was on the top floor.

As the juice went into his cell's battery, bringing it back to life, the number of texts he'd received was over one hundred. Not unusual after being away for so long. What was unusual to him was the person who'd sent five of the messages.

Dylan.

Cam and his brother were tight. He knew Dylan better than

anyone. Dylan didn't send multiple texts. One. That was all. Then his brother waited patiently for a response.

Cam clicked on the last message from Dylan and his jaw clenched.

Erica has been kidnapped.

* * * *

6:39 p.m., Friday – TBK Tower, Destiny, Colorado

Dylan was glad to see the text from Cam that had just popped up on his cell's screen. "Cam's in town. He cut his vacation short. He's headed here now."

"We can use all hands on deck," Jason said.

Time was ticking away and every second was like a bullet to Dylan's gut.

Erica was gone and in danger.

Emotions blasted through him like a storm. Images of her being tortured and raped floated in his mind over and over. The next horrific vision had him curling his hands into tight fists.

She can't be dead. If I could just hold her, put my arms around her, tell her everything is going to be okay...

"It's six forty-five," Jason announced, giving another fifteen-minute warning.

Dylan shook his head, trying to clear his mind. Emotions were useless. He had to act. He had to find her. The only thing that would help him was his training. Latching onto his logic, he typed away, searching for any electronic breadcrumb that he could find on his monitor.

"Call your brother," he told Scott. "See how long before he and the Texans get here."

Scott nodded, grabbing his cell.

Jason was once again pacing around the large table. "You have to make this happen, Dylan. I don't have any leads."

"I will," he stated flatly, feeling his intensity rise. "I'm uploading some files to the secure server. Cam can get to work on them when he arrives. When Scott's brother and the Texans show up, they can help, too."

Cam knew more than a little about hacking. The truth that had been kept under wraps for years was that Cam had hacked into their high school's computer network when he was a sophomore. He'd been caught, thankfully. Their two dads had brought down the hammer, and that had been the turning point in his brother's life that eventually led him to law school. Cam was the only man he truly trusted in the courtroom or anywhere else, especially with something this sensitive. He and Cam had each other's backs always.

Jason was right. Erica needed all hands on deck. Having Cam here was something he needed, too.

Staring at a monitor, Scott shook his head. "This has Kip Lunceford's fingerprints all over it."

Jason hit the table with his fists creating a loud bang. "Damn it, I don't need another maniac suspect to deal with. Mitrofanov is Destiny's Most Wanted. He has to be behind this. Not Lunceford. For the love of God, the bastard is in prison." The sheriff was on edge, like all of them. Time was ticking away and they were no closer to finding Erica than they had been when they'd started the cyber search for the needle in the Internet's haystack.

Dylan wasn't about to remind Jason that Niklaus Mitrofanov, a Russian mafia father, had paid a dirty politician to get a meeting with Lunceford at the prison. The sheriff knew it. They all did. All the charges against Mitrofanov had been dropped after the deaths of two state witnesses. Jason was working hard to uncover a link in the murders to the mobster. The Russian had a grudge against Destiny. His son had been killed here. Dylan had known many Mitrofanov types during his days in the Agency. Niklaus had been a lowly pickpocket back in Russia. He'd served time. When he'd gotten to the

States, the man's ambition had propelled him to his current status as kingpin of a large organization. Niklaus would never stop until the city was nothing but ruble or he was dead. If the bastard had anything to do with Erica's disappearance, Dylan would find him and make sure the Russian joined his son in the grave.

Though Dylan found it hard to believe that Lunceford could have any reach now, after the new warden at the maximum-security prison had locked the lunatic up so tight, he knew the most impossible things often could happen given enough time and will. "What fingerprints of Kip's are you seeing, Scott?"

"Believe it or not, any coder has a certain style that is identifiable to other techs," Scott said. "See here." Knight pointed to a line on the monitor in front of Dylan. "This sequence isn't really part of the code. It's more of a placeholder."

Gen1usKLw1ns.

Dylan pondered the strange jumble, hoping to discover something, anything, that would point to Erica's whereabouts.

* * * *

10:02 a.m., Friday – on the side of a highway

Erica felt the car stop.

She moaned as loud as she could, praying someone would hear her. But the sirens continued on, fading as the unseen police car passed her abductors' vehicle.

I'm going to die.

Chapter Two

6:47 p.m., Friday – TBK Tower, Destiny, Colorado

Dylan stared at his monitor. "I've seen this before in lines of Kip Lunceford's malicious code we discovered in the TBK network."

Scott nodded. "It's one of several of the bastard's calling cards."

Kip Lunceford, what are you up to?

Dylan's normally regimented mind was betraying him. Speculation was part of his job. Always had been. Gather facts. Make deductions. Act. More facts. More deductions until the mission objective was achieved, whether target or extraction. But the visions of Erica that kept creeping into his head were clouding his judgment.

For Dylan, a cut-and-dried, by-the-book, systematic life made sense of a senseless world. He was, at his heart, an agent of death. Yes, all his targets had deserved their demise—more than deserved—but killing changed a man bit by bit. After his first kill, an Al-Qaeda stateside operative, several Jack Daniel's bottles had comforted him for three days.

The next mission, two bottles and two days.

The next, a single bottle and a single day.

Since then, he'd never touched a drop of alcohol, knowing its impact on him.

"Looks like the hacker who sent the ransom e-mail has slipped away to another server farm. Damn." Scott's tone gave a clear signal that his hope to find Erica alive was disappearing fast. "This is a big provider, too."

Dylan felt his gut tighten. Whoever was behind Erica's

abduction—Kip, Niklaus, or some other guy—he was extremely talented. Right now an image of Erica glassy-eyed and unbreathing was clawing at the back of his mind. For the first time in years, he craved the dullness Jack Daniel's could bring.

"Keep looking, Scott," he instructed. "We're not giving up. There's something here that will help us find her."

Scott nodded.

Dylan wasn't a praying man, but for the first time since childhood, he begged God for a favor.

Save her.

* * * *

10:05 a.m., Friday – three hours from Destiny, Colorado

As the car began to roll again, even with the hood over her head, Erica felt tears roll down her cheeks.

There were so many things she wished she'd said to Reed and Sawyer. They'd been her only family after their parents died. She was so happy that her brothers had found love with Nicole.

Eric and Scott had been the best bosses, friends, and advisors a woman could ask for. She smiled weakly, thrilled they'd found Megan.

Even the Stones, the three who rounded out the orphan posse, had found true love in Amber.

What have I found? Only heartache. She would never have her own family. No kids. Nothing. Her dream of Dylan and Cam? *Just a dream.*

Death was gunning for her. Two previous events had made that clear.

The first event had been back at TBK where she'd made the biggest mistake in her life. She could've been killed if Megan and Gretchen hadn't shoved down their fear and used their heads. Unlike she'd done. Those women had been so brave and smart.

I need to do the same if I have any chance of surviving this.

The second attempt had been up at her brothers' cabin. A crazy bitch from Chicago who wanted Nicole dead had come close to shooting Erica if not for a lucky twist of fate.

This one—the third in the Reaper's attempts—was likely to succeed in placing her in the grave.

Her heart was still racing as dread swamped every one of her conscious thoughts.

She wasn't sure where these criminals were taking her or how long she'd been their prisoner, but she could tell by the popping of her ears that they were descending. This had to be a much lower elevation than Destiny, her hometown in Colorado.

Had there been anything she could've done to prevent this from happening?

She'd arrived at work early, as per normal, at seven in the morning. It was one of several of her routines she'd been able to continue these past few months. Some of her other daily procedures were hit and miss.

God, why can't I let go of the past? She knew she needed to, but only time would allow her to heal.

Time? She wasn't sure she had much more of it. Still inside the trunk, her mind spun with a million thoughts.

Her whole world had been flipped on its head when an employee had made it past her desk by coercing her to comply with a pistol aimed at her head. She'd almost gotten everyone killed, especially Megan.

Kip Lunceford, Megan's ex, had been behind the whole mess.

Could my kidnapping be a part of the same scheme by Kip? How?

He was still in prison in solitary confinement. She didn't think it was possible this could be connected. Besides, the men who'd taken her had distinct Russian accents. They had to be connected to the Mitrofanov syndicate that Sheriff Jason Wolfe was trying to bring down. Nicole, her brothers' fiancée and also the sheriff's new deputy, was helping him build the case.

This couldn't be connected to Kip Lunceford. Could it?

* * * *

6:52 p.m., Friday – TBK Tower, Destiny, Colorado

Dylan was hitting too many dead ends. If he didn't figure out something soon, Scott might have to transfer the ransom that had been demanded in the e-mail.

"Scott, any clue what this odd placeholder in the code you mentioned might mean?" Jason asked. "Give me something to go on. Anything."

The billionaire shrugged.

"I think I might know." Dylan nodded. "The dollar sign is a word divider. The number one is—"

Cameron rushed through the door and into the room. "What do we know? How can I help? Do we know where or who took Erica?" His face was dark with concern.

Dylan was relieved some that Cam was here, but he held up his hand to him. "Hold up for a sec."

Scott turned to him. "I still can't make heads or tails out of this placeholder even if the dollar sign is a word divider. The only thing that might make sense is the 'KL' stands for Kip Lunceford."

"That definitely is the case," Dylan told him. "Kip is arrogant."

"Yes." Scott nodded. "He's the most arrogant, self-absorbed lunatic I've ever known."

He looked at his screen and realized another country had popped up. "I just found a server in the Ukraine, fellows." *How many rabbit holes are in this?*

"On it, Dylan," Cam said, taking a seat at one of the free computers.

"You're right, Sheriff," he continued. "*KL* is Kip Lunceford. Now, replace the *1* with the letter *i* and that's the message."

Scott said aloud what he'd already figured out. "Genius Kip Lunceford wins. What an asshole."

"That's Kip," Jason said, his face dark red.

"Found it," Cam said. "The e-mail came from Vernal, Utah."

"Hold on." He shook his head. "I just sent you what I found. Casper, Wyoming."

"What does that mean?" Jason asked.

"One might be the origination point," he said, realizing how complicated the rescue mission was becoming. "The other is just a mirror to get us off the scent."

"Wait," Cam said. "Here's a third. A suburb in Denver."

Scott shook his head. "What if they're all just repeaters and the real location is masked?"

"That might be true," Cam acknowledged.

"But it's all we have to go on. There's nothing more to do here. The code has dried up." Dylan stood, knowing it was time for him to take charge. He was the best in mission planning, and this mission meant life or death to Erica. "We're running out of time before TBK is supposed to make the first wire transfer. We need three teams to go to all these locations."

"I've got the physical address for the one in Vernal," Cam said. "Sending it now."

"Got it." Scott typed on his iPad. "That's five and a half hours from Destiny. We need to go now."

"The Denver and Casper addresses are about the same," Dylan said.

Scott stood. "Give us our orders, Dylan."

"I'm going with you, too," Cam stated firmly.

Dylan couldn't blame his brother. He, too, cared about Erica. There wasn't another man he wanted by his side more for this mission than Cam.

* * * *

11:10 a.m., Friday – four hours from Destiny, Colorado

Erica's guilty wounds continued to burn. Still inside the trunk, her mind wouldn't settle. Though mental not physical, her wounds had been given to her by Kip Lunceford and his gun-totting pawn.

Everyone, including Megan, told her that she'd done nothing wrong. She just hadn't been able to accept that. Over and over, she'd wrestled with the events of that day. She'd been paralyzed by fear. Human? Yes. But it didn't help to ease her guilt.

Her only saving grace had been the routines she'd been able to continue.

Arrive early at TBK. Park the car. Head over to Blue's Diner. Get a bagel and a cup of coffee. Walk down West Street. Reach up and touch the toe of The Green Dragon statue for luck. Back to TBK. Up the elevator. Think about the day's tasks—*not about what happened before.* Get to work.

That had seen Erica through her guilty haze—*until today.*

Halfway through her morning steps, right before she had a chance to touch the lucky toe, the two bruisers had jumped her. Her bagel, coffee, and laptop had fallen to the sidewalk when they'd gagged her. They'd put the hood on her and threw her in their trunk before she had a chance to fight or scream.

She remembered seeing Hiro Phong across the street unlocking the door to his restaurant, but he'd had his back to her and her abductors. No one else was on the streets that early.

I've got to stop this. No more negative thoughts.

* * * *

6:55 p.m., Friday – TBK Tower, Destiny, Colorado

Dylan's Glock was holstered to his side under his suit coat. It was time to take this mission to the field. His gun needed to be in his hand firing at the people responsible for Erica's kidnapping. But which of the three locations was she being held? Casper? Vernal? Denver?

Why didn't I tell Erica she was beautiful?

This rescue mission needed to be underway and in the field already—not in a conference room in front of a computer.

"Fuck," he said. "Where are the Texans? We need to get on the road—now."

Scott and Jason turned to him, making him wish he had better control of his emotions. But he wasn't in control. Not when it came to Erica.

Scott looked down at his iPad. "They're here. Security just sent them up."

* * * *

12:21 p.m., Friday – an industrial district of Denver, Colorado

Erica remembered her talks with Nicole, and in particular one certain conversation with her soon-to-be sister-in-law.

"Self-defense begins with your mind," Nicole had said. "Don't let it run away from you. Keep it reined in. Start thinking about your next move and the one after that and the one after that."

Okay. Think. What can I do?

They would have to untie her sometime. When they did, she could kick them in the balls and run. But there were two of them. That likely wasn't going to work.

What then?

She thought about a certain ex-CIA agent. What would Dylan do? If anyone would know how to get out of this mess, it would be him. God, how she wished the sexy man was here right now. But he wasn't. Only her.

She felt the car come to a stop.

Her pulse increased.

She vowed to take one step at a time and to look for an opportunity to escape.

If they took off the hood, she would be able to see.

If they took off the gag, she'd be able to scream.

Right now, she had to wait and stay calm.

Breathe.

The engine stopped.

Now, she could hear her kidnappers.

"Time to get our package to the boss," one of them said in a thick Russian accent.

Boss? She needed information. The more she could learn the better her chances of getting out alive.

The mobsters exited the car with two door slams that shook the entire vehicle.

She heard the trunk lid open.

The hood came off.

Her eyes took a second to focus.

The bald one with two arms full of tats grinned wickedly. "How was the ride, miss?"

"Be careful with this one, Karl." The other bastard had a head full of hair. There was a deep, dark scar that ran from the bottom of his right eye and down his cheek. "Look at the fire in our little sparrow's eyes."

Karl grinned. "She's definitely a fighter, Vlad."

Damn right, I am.

Fighting the trembles inside her, she made a vow to herself.

I will not die today.

* * * *

6:59 p.m., Friday – TBK Tower, Destiny, Colorado

Dylan's pulse was hot in his veins. *Time to go get her back. Time to kill the motherfucker who took her away.*

The Texans, Matt Dixon and Sean MacCabe, two former CIA associates he'd worked with in the field years ago, walked into the conference room with Scott's brother Eric. Following close behind were Erica's brothers and Nicole.

"Have you found our sister?" Sawyer rushed in, worry all over his face.

"We have three possibilities," Jason told them. "Dylan thinks he's in charge here, but he's not. I am. I'm the law."

He liked Jason. "You're way out of your league here, Sheriff. Whoever has taken Erica is a professional. Whoever sent the ransom note is also. If she has any chance of survival, this has to be handled by the best, and the best happens to be me and the Texans."

"Fine, but you better know I'm the one with the badge."

Dylan respected Jason's authority, but this was Erica. She was too important to him to let anyone else take the lead. "Sheriff, you and Matt can go to one location."

"You're not going to get my sister without me and Sawyer." By the look on Reed's face, he knew the man meant business.

Sawyer nodded his agreement.

"We're all going," Nicole said. "Jason is sheriff. I'm the deputy. Case closed. How do we proceed?"

Dylan liked the deputy's moxie. And she'd made it clear to him, back when the Russians were after her, that she was good with her gun. Very good.

He studied the rest of the team.

In a flash, he had the mission devised in his head. "Scott and Eric need to stay here in case the transfer has to go through."

"We're on the job," Scott answered.

Dylan knew the Knight brothers would gladly pay the ransom to get Erica back, but he hated that the bastard kidnappers would get all that money. "My associates at the Federal Reserve are ready on their end to track the funds."

"I'll talk to my contacts to see what we can do," Eric said.

Reed put his arm around Nicole. "Hopefully, we'll find Erica before you have to make the transfer."

This has to work. He continued giving the orders. "Matt will be the lead for the Casper operation. Reed and Nicole will be on that team. Sean will lead the team to Vernal. That'll be Sawyer and Jason. Cam, you're with me. We'll head to Denver." His brother was as good a shot as any agent he'd ever known. "Keep your heads clear. We'll stay in touch via cell. Eric and Scott will act as our command base. Everyone understand what your roles are?"

"We got it," Cam answered, heading out the door.

"Let's go," he said to the others before following his brother.

* * * *

12:01 a.m., Saturday – an empty warehouse in Denver, Colorado

Erica's muscles ached from being tied up in the trunk of the car for so long and to the chair, but she wasn't about to complain to her abductors. God, how long had it been since they brought her here? The sun had been high in the sky when they took her into this place. It had been down for several hours. It must be getting really late.

The day was almost over—a day that had been a complete nightmare. What would tomorrow bring? Would she survive?

By now, everyone in Destiny had to know she was missing. Were they trying to find her? She was sure they must be. But what chance would they have in finding her? No one had seen her this morning. There were no clues for them to follow. She was completely freaked out, but who wouldn't be? Her abductors hadn't touched her. Did that mean they needed her for some other reason? A ransom perhaps?

Bribery? She wasn't sure, but she knew if anyone could find her, it would be Dylan and Cam Strange. The two men, though different in so many ways, had unique skills to uncover the truth. *Please, God, let them find me.*

Her captors reminded her of serial killers from horror flicks—Norman Bates and Freddy Krueger. Vlad and Karl. To keep her mind from slipping into despair, she'd silently named the pair "Humpty" and "Dumpty."

Humpty was the one with all the tats. Dumpty had that terrifying scar on his face. Since Dumpty had left over an hour ago to get food, Humpty had been staring at her the whole time, which was creeping her out. They'd brought her into this empty warehouse and tied her to a chair.

Humpty stood. "Got to drain the main vein, babe. Don't worry. I'll be right back." He laughed before exiting.

Now's your chance. She tried to work her ankles and wrists free, but the ropes wouldn't budge. In the movies, people were tied up close to a pole or wall with a jagged edge or nail. She didn't catch that break. The two Russians had placed the chair in the middle of the space. No wall. No pole. Nothing to help her get the ropes off.

Was anyone coming for her? They just had to be. At least trying to find her. Please God, help them. Help me.

Dumpty came in through the door, his arms loaded with two pizza boxes and a bottle of vodka. "I bet you're hungry, aren't you, sweetheart?"

She didn't answer. The look in his eyes reminded her of how Felix had looked that day back in the TBK Tower. Crazed. *Got to tread carefully.*

Humpty came back from the bathroom. "I'm fucking starving. I hope you got triple meat."

His comrade nodded. "You know what would go better with dinner?" More Norman Bates than Dumpty at the moment, his lusty gaze landed on her like a branding iron.

"We're not supposed to touch her, Vlad," Karl said without much conviction in his voice.

It still gave her hope. Someone else was pulling the strings. They had a boss to answer to. But whoever was in charge wasn't here. She wasn't sure these two would follow orders to the letter anyway.

"Guys, I wouldn't mind some pizza," she said, hoping to pull them out of their wicked ideas for her.

"We deserve this, Karl." Vlad set the boxes of pizza down and walked over to her with the vodka. "Better prime the pump."

Karl smiled. *God, I wished I'd thought of something else to call him.* "I suppose we do deserve a little fun on this job."

"Fuck right, we do." The scarred man stared down at her. "How about a drink, honey?"

She shook her head.

His eyes narrowed as his lips thinned. "You will drink or you will regret what I will do to you."

"Okay. Okay." Her panic, which had been somewhat under control, was once again rising inside her. *Breathe.* Impossible to do at the moment, but she had to try. It was her only hope.

"Open your mouth, babe," the tat-armed man said.

She parted her lips slightly.

"Wider, bitch," the other monster ordered.

When she did, he grabbed her by the hair and pulled, forcing her face to the ceiling. Vlad poured the vodka down her throat until she thought she might gag.

"That's a pretty slut," the creep said, releasing her hair and bringing his hand to her breast.

Instinct kicked in, and she spewed the vodka into his face.

"Fucking cunt." Vlad backhanded her across the mouth.

She tasted blood on her lips. Her mind was spinning as fear shook her to her core. And then she felt a slight bit of calm come over her. Odd, but true. She imagined what Nicole would do in this situation. She would be strong. She would constantly weigh her options.

Erica decided it was best to try to act more like Nicole, like Megan, like Gretchen.

Being mauled disgusted her, but if she could make them believe she was compliant, they might loosen her restraints. Then she might have a chance to make a move to escape.

"Sorry," she said in the sweetest tone she could roll out. "My drink of choice has always been wine over vodka." She needed an advantage. She gathered her courage. "Please take it slow with me, fellows. We're all starving. Karl just said so. Shouldn't we eat first, Vlad?" She used their names, hoping to get into their heads.

"Now that's more like it, sparrow." Vlad's hands moved down her shoulders. "I want to see your tits."

"Me, too," Karl said, sending a chill through her body. "If we're going to be our best with this one, we should eat."

"True, but we can get our dicks revved up by getting a peek at our dessert while we dine." Vlad pulled out a switchblade from his pocket. "Pretty little sparrow." He brought the blade up to her chin, and she felt her heart stop. "Don't worry, babe. I wouldn't dare mar your face. The boss would have my balls on a platter if I did. But I will rip you apart with my cock." Using his knife, he split her top and bra, exposing her breasts. The cold air hit her naked skin like a razor.

"Fuck, those tits are something else." Karl took a swig on the bottle of vodka, but his eyes never left her chest. He handed it to Vlad, who took a long swallow of the white liquor.

She closed her eyes, unable to be brave any longer. "Please, can't we eat first?" Her voice sounded so weak and tiny.

"Yes, sparrow," Vlad said in a sickening voice. "I'm going to bite down on these delicious tits."

Karl snorted. "She's our meal, yes?"

"Yes."

Vlad and Karl were going to rape her and there wasn't a thing she could do about it. Better rape than death, but still rape.

They are Humpty and Dumpty. They are Humpty and Dumpty.

The mantra didn't help this time. Dread sunk down into her gut like a lead weight, crushing her hope for survival.

God, help me.

She heard a door open. She saw Karl and Vlad place the barrels of their guns to her head.

Erica peered into the shadows by the doorway and saw the two men she'd been praying would come to her rescue. Dylan and Cam were armed and ready.

Vlad's face turned grim as Dylan and Cam came into view. "Move one inch closer, assholes, and this little sparrow is dead."

Chapter Three

12:12 a.m., Saturday – an empty warehouse in Denver, Colorado

Cameron felt a mix of relief and rage—relief at finding Erica alive in a chair and rage at seeing the motherfuckers who had taken her from Destiny. The pricks had stripped her from the waist up. Had they raped her? His pulse burned like lava in his veins. Seeing them holding their guns to her head was causing his heart to thud hard in his chest. Adrenaline was coursing through his body to act, but he and Dylan had to be smart. She must survive this night.

The bastard with the scar sneered. "Lower your weapons and put your hands up."

"You're clearly in charge here," Dylan said in a flat tone.

Cam knew his brother was only buying time by talking, trying to get the two men off guard.

"You assholes better do what we say," the one with the tats barked at him.

Dylan turned to Cam. "You take out Tat," he whispered.

He nodded, keeping his finger on the trigger.

The two dicks smirked.

"We said drop you weapons." The bastard swung his weapon away from Erica's head to their direction.

"Now!" Dylan yelled.

They both fired their guns at Erica's kidnappers. The bullets hit their marks, delivering instant mortal wounds in the two assholes. The thugs fell to the ground, their eyes wide in glassy-dead surprise.

"Oh my God," Erica said, tears streaming down her cheeks.

"You're here."

He and Dylan ran to her.

In a flash they had her out of her restraints and in their arms.

Unable to hold back his overwhelming emotions, Cam kissed her. She melted into him, surrendering her lips to his.

Dylan took off his jacket and placed it around her. "Let's get her out of here to somewhere secure. Then we can call the others. My bet is these two aren't the only ones involved in this."

"They aren't." Erica's big blue eyes glistened from teardrops. "They mentioned a boss."

Cam hauled Erica up into his arms. She placed her arms around his neck. He followed Dylan, who had his gun in his hand, out of the warehouse.

* * * *

11:57 p.m., Saturday – a highway four hours from Destiny, Colorado

Long days and nights were something Dylan knew quite well, but the past forty-eight hours had been utter hell.

Erica was safe. They'd won the most important battle, even if the ten million dollars that Scott had sent to the Russian market vanished in a few seconds. That fact seemed to indicate Niklaus Mitrofanov as the culprit calling the shots. The other purchases were legit, which was surprising. Real companies. The Knights could sell their shares in the next couple of days and get most of their money back. He wasn't happy that the Russian had netted so much money, but he was glad that the heat was off of Erica. There would be no reason for the mobster to come after her again. Once back in Destiny, Dylan would help Jason bring down Mitrofanov and try to recover Eric and Scott's ten million.

A current pop love ballad drifted out of the Mercedes's speakers. Normally, Dylan traveled without music, better to stay alert and on guard, but Erica's shivering had moved Cameron to turn on SiriusXM.

His brother had incredibly good instincts in sensing what she needed. Cam was taking good care of Erica, extremely good care. She seemed to relax a little listening to the tunes. Only fifteen minutes into the drive back to Destiny, she finally dozed off. Thank God. She deserved a little respite from all she'd gone through.

The images of those two motherfuckers were burned into his mind. They were just Mitrofanov's muscle. Whatever it took, Dylan was going to make the man pay for what he'd done to Erica.

Behind the wheel of Cam's car, Dylan glanced over at Erica. She was asleep in his brother's arms. From the gentle breathing he heard from Cam, Dylan could tell that he, too, had nodded off. Understandable, since the long amount of time they'd spent with Denver PD. Giving their statements had taken many hours. They'd still be there if he and the Texans hadn't called in a few favors from old associates at the Agency.

The sun was just now going down. Four more hours until they reached home.

Home?

Destiny was a unique place. People were accepted there. He and Cam had grown up in a typical family in the town, unlike most places in the world where there was one mom and one dad living in the same house.

There had been eight people in the Strange household. Four children. Four parents. He and Cam had two younger sisters, twins, but as different as night and day. Both were twenty-five and working on their graduate degrees, Celeste on her MBA and Caitlin on her psychology degree. He missed them. Would they come back to Destiny after graduation? He thought Celeste would, but he wasn't sure about Caitlin.

When he and Cam had been younger, they'd talked about what it would be like to start a family together. But that was a long time ago before the CIA had recruited him after his tour had ended in the military.

He turned off the interstate and onto Highway F, which would take them almost all the way into Destiny. *Four more hours to go.*

He dared another glance at Erica. Staring at her was so fucking inappropriate. He didn't deserve her. Not after all the blood he'd spilled. Too much blood.

He moved his attention back to the road.

"How are you doing?" Erica said softly, leaning up from Cam, who was still asleep.

"I should be asking you that. Not the other way around." He wanted to put his arm around her and pull her into him. But he didn't. She deserved someone like Cam, not someone like him.

"Better. How long was I out?"

"Fifteen minutes, tops. Go back to sleep. We still have a lot of road to cover."

"I'd rather keep my eyes open, if you don't mind. It beats being in the trunk of a car with a hood over your head." She laughed weakly, which crushed him.

Even after all that had happened to her, she was trying to grab onto any semblance of light. Erica was stronger than even she knew.

"I wanted to thank you, Dylan."

Hearing his name from her sweet lips sparked another flood of longing, not just for sex, but also for a connection—one that was honest, open, and real. "No need. I'm head of TBK security. It's my job."

She sighed. "I know, but that wasn't what I wanted to thank you for."

"Oh?" *Tell her she's beautiful. Now's your chance.* "What?"

"For the self-defense lessons. For the gun range training."

"I don't understand, Erica."

She put her hand on his forearm. Her tender touch fueled his already out-of-control emotions to overflowing. "When I was sure I wasn't going to make it out alive and was ready to give up, your words came back to me. Yours and Nicole's. That's what kept me sane and kept me hoping that I would survive."

"You did survive," he told her, placing his hand over her delicate fingers. "You did good."

"I survived because of you and Cam. If you hadn't shown up when you did…they were going to…"

"It's okay. They didn't."

This was one fucked-up mess, and Erica was right in the middle of it.

She leaned her head into his shoulder and looked up at him with her sky blue eyes. "I'd like to resume my training, if that's okay with you."

Okay? More than okay. "We'll start back on Monday. You should rest for the remainder of the weekend."

"Once again, I was such a fool." The melancholy in her tone cut him like a knife. "As you know, I'm still uncomfortable with a gun. I almost put it in my purse yesterday morning, but I didn't. What's the use in going to the gun range in the Knights' basement to work on my shooting if I'm afraid to have it on me when you're not around?"

"Don't talk about yourself that way," he stated firmly. "First of all, those creeps were professionals. The gun wouldn't have given you an advantage, in fact, it might've gotten you killed."

"You're just saying that to make me feel better. You and I both know I should've had it on me."

Erica's nature was to be upbeat and happy. She'd suffered so much and had been changed by all the turn of events. God, who wouldn't be changed by them?

"I don't let anyone tear down people I care about, and that includes when they are doing it to themselves like you are now. Understand?"

She blinked. "You care about me, Dylan?"

Damn it. How did I let that slip out? "Go back to sleep, Erica.

This is a long drive."

She nodded and then closed her eyes. It wasn't long before her breathing slowed, letting him know she'd dozed off again. His emotions for her were pegging the needle, which was so unfamiliar to him. Balance was his norm. Reason. Logic. He took a deep breath and let it out slowly, trying to rein in his mind. With her head still on his shoulder and her sweet scent wafting up into his nostrils, it didn't work. Couldn't work.

Get a grip on yourself, agent.

He couldn't stop sneaking a peek away from the road ahead to the gorgeous woman between him and Cam. He wanted her. Really wanted her. Had for a very long time, just like Cam.

The pro side of the list on why he should pursue Erica was long.

She brought out something buried deep in him that he'd thought would never see the light of day. *Hope.* Erica could look at him and he would feel the hardness around his heart soften. She would speak to him and the rage clawing at his soul would weaken. Her touch made the darkness inside him lighten. He had no doubt the sex would be fucking amazing. Her body had the curves, the softness he would enjoy conquering. Erica was from Destiny. She'd been trained as a submissive at the club. Her family had been poly, too, just like his and Cam's. She fit perfectly into what kind of woman he and Cam could love and share. And there were even more pros down the list.

But the con side was just as long.

Most of the cons were images that floated in his head. The visions that haunted him were the faces of targets he'd successfully taken out during his time at the Agency. He was a killer, and a damn good one. He would still be killing at the CIA had it not been for his last mission. His gut tightened, recalling that failure.

"You okay, Dylan?" Cam's question helped him break free of that fateful night.

"Good," he said in a hushed tone. "She's fallen back to sleep."

"I see that. You want me to drive so you can get some rest?"

He shook head. "I got this."

"Wrong," Cam's tone sharpened. "*We* got this. You and me."

He knew his brother was trying to get him to open up, to share his feelings, but he couldn't. Not about Erica. Not now. "You did good tonight, bro."

"Fuck, Dylan. Stop changing the subject. Erica needs us. Not just for now but for a long time. You do see that, don't you?"

"This isn't the time to repeat your diatribe about why Erica Coleman is for us, Cam."

"When is the right time? Tomorrow? The next day? The day after that? Next week? Next month?"

Once again, his emotions were bubbling up to the surface, and all of them about Erica. "Don't give me your lawyer closing argument. I'm not a judge or jury or client."

"Wrong again. You get to decide if Erica is worth fighting for."

"What the hell do you mean? We won the fight. The bad guys lost. She's safe."

"You've got to stop pushing everyone away that you care about. You deserve happiness as much as anyone. So do I. And so does she." Cam looked at Erica, his eyes full of caring. "She's suffered so much."

"I know," he said, hating the pain she carried. Yes, she and Cam deserved happiness, deserved each other. Dylan wanted to tell his brother why he didn't, but those details were classified.

"You and I can help her," Cam continued, trying to persuade him. God, he loved his brother. "She needs us. We can build a real family with her."

"I agree." *And I need her.* He mentally added that to the list. It fit in both the pro and con columns for different reasons. "Let's get back to Destiny and take things one step at a time, okay?"

"You're willing to take some steps for her?" Cam asked, the excitement in his voice obvious.

"Patience, bro. I'm willing to help her." A plan formed in his mind, a plan that would give two of the most important people in his life a chance at happiness. He'd never lied to Cameron. *If it means happiness for him and Erica, then I'll do it no matter how guilty it makes me feel. No matter the heartbreak I'll have to suffer.*

Chapter Four

4:03 a.m., Sunday – Blue's Diner, Destiny, Colorado

Erica felt the car come to a stop, and in her mind she was back in the trunk listening to the sirens fading off in the distance. She opened her eyes, feeling her pulse pound hard in her veins.

She wasn't in the trunk, and there were no sirens. She was between Dylan and Cam, and all she could hear was the music coming from the car's speakers.

She looked out the windshield. Dylan had parked the car in front of Blue's Diner. "What are we doing here?"

Strangely, the lights were on inside the restaurant. It was two more hours before the place opened up.

"While you were sleeping, sweetheart, your brothers called. They can't wait to see you. Aunt Alice opened up early for this celebration." Cam brushed the hair out of her eyes.

Dylan and Cam's aunt and uncles were some of the sweetest people in Destiny. Alice Blue knew how to keep her husbands in line. Eddie and Curtis worshiped the ground the woman walked on. They had three adult children, and their daughter, Phoebe, was one of Erica's closest friends. Her brothers were as opposite as they come. Corey Blue was a US Marshal and Shane was serving time for drug possession.

"By the number of cars parked around the place, it looks like there are several people who want to welcome you back," Dylan said in his typical factual tone, pulling the key out of the ignition.

The motor's hum and radio's music, which had lulled Erica to sleep, quieted.

Being welcomed by a crowd wasn't something she wanted to face, but how could she not? So many had helped find her so that Dylan and Cam could come to her rescue. She owed it to the whole town to put on a brave face. More importantly, she wanted to see her brothers.

She took a deep breath. "Let's go."

Walking between Dylan and Cam, she entered Blue's. The diner was packed. Not a single seat was open.

Had all of Destiny shown up this early just for her? A large banner was strung up to the ceiling with the words "Welcome Home, Erica."

Sawyer and Reed ran to her, sweeping her up in their arms. She sobbed, letting the tears flow.

"Sis, you're here," Reed choked out.

"You're safe." Though Sawyer's eyes brimmed with tears, not a single drop fell. Her brothers were tough. They'd helped her through the loss of their parents. God, how much more did her family have to suffer?

It felt so good to be home in Destiny. She couldn't seem to compose herself. More tears.

Nicole joined her brothers in hugging her. "Erica, I was right. You're a very strong woman."

She didn't feel strong. Quite the opposite in fact. But she wasn't about to let anyone see her crumble. Looking around the room, she saw so many familiar smiling faces. Keeping a secret in Destiny just wasn't possible. She smiled, knowing the phones must've been ringing all night.

"I hope you are hungry, Erica." Alice came up, wiping her eyes. And then the dear woman gave her a big hug.

More hugs came from her loved ones and neighbors.

Phoebe, Alice's daughter, came up next with her two brothers, Corey and Shane.

Erica was shocked to see Shane. "Are you really out?" she asked him.

"Yes. I made my parole." Shane's blue eyes were just as devilish as they'd ever been. "How do I look?" he asked with a wink. He wore a buzz cut, which was different than before.

"Simply marvelous, darling," she teased. "The past three years have been good to you."

Shane rubbed his head. "Wait until my dark hair grows out. The women around here won't have a chance."

"Same old Shane," Jason said as he walked up next to her.

"Don't start, Sheriff." Phoebe frowned.

Jason shrugged. "Your brother keeps out of trouble, we won't have any issues." The sheriff turned to Corey, Phoebe's other brother. "How are you doing?"

"I'm good, Sheriff." Corey was a US Marshal. Phoebe was an attorney. Shane was the black sheep of the Blue family, but also the one everyone in town, except Jason, loved.

The Texans ran up to her.

Matt smiled and gave her a hug. "It's good to have you back, Erica."

"Really good," Sean added.

Dylan and Cam had told her how the Texans were part of her search team. "I understand you guys helped find me. Thank you."

"We're not done yet," Matt said. "We still think the hacker is connected to your abduction."

Sean looked at Dylan and Jason. "We're close to finding his location."

"Let's talk soon. I want to know what you've found out so far. Keep me up to date on everything," Dylan told him.

Reed tapped a glass with a knife. "May I have your attention?" The crowd settled down immediately, everyone turning their attention to her brother. "I'd like to offer a toast to Destiny's favorite daughter, Erica Coleman, my little sister."

Applause broke out in the room along with several whistles and happy shouts.

"Everyone, please sit down now," Alice said. "Curtis and Eddie have been slaving away in the kitchen for you. I don't want the food to get cold."

Erica felt her fatigue from the top of her head to the bottom of her feet as she sat down in the center booth. Even more, she felt her hunger. She was starving. The aromas filling the room got her stomach to growling. The biscuits at Blue's were the best in the state.

She was between Dylan and Cam in the booth, and that eased some of her anxiety as more people filed by with their sweet words.

Alice poured them all coffee. "I've got your favorites set up," she told them. "And not that silly bagel you eat during the week, Erica. This is the big breakfast. Bacon and eggs. Biscuits and gravy. Followed by hot pancakes."

After everyone was chowing down on the delicious meal the Blues had prepared, the line of people greeting her stopped for a bit.

Dylan leaned over. "Eat up, Erica. I know these people. They are ready to go until sunup. But you're exhausted."

"Yes, you are." Cam touched her cheek. "I can see it in your eyes."

"We're going to take you home," Dylan said.

Her gut tightened. "I really don't want to be alone."

"We're not going to leave you, sweetheart." Cam's fingertips traced her face. "We'll stay the whole time, on guard, while you sleep. I don't care if it's twenty-four hours."

"We want you to get completely rested." She gazed at her own reflection in Dylan's sunglasses. He grabbed her hand. "And the only way you are going to be able to do that is if we are there with you."

"But you're tired, too." How could she ask them to do more than they'd already done? "I can see if Nicole and my brothers can come stay at my house."

Dylan smiled. "I never sleep with both eyes closed, honey."

"Who would know?" Cam shook his head. "You never take off those damn sunglasses."

She laughed.

Matt and Sean, the two Texans Dylan had brought to TBK to weed out Kip Lunceford's code, walked up to their booth.

"Mind if we join you for a second?" Matt asked.

Cam motioned to the other side of the booth. "Have a seat. What have you found out about the hacker?"

"Did you locate the bastard yet?" Dylan asked, clearly back on the job as head of security.

Matt shook his head. "This guy is good. The warehouse we found in Wyoming was loaded to the brim with the best computers available."

"Same in Utah," Sean said. "We're dealing with a pro. I think we almost got the guy. There was a pot of coffee that was still warm to the touch when we got there. I checked the perimeter. Nothing. Following protocols, I set up a stakeout with local authorities in case the dude returned. They were happy to help after I let them talk to Mr. Black at the Agency."

By the look on Dylan's face, it was clear he knew the person, too. How far up in the CIA had they gone to find and rescue her? Apparently, pretty high.

Matt nodded. "I did the same in Wyoming. We'll catch the hacker eventually, and that will lead us to Mitrofanov."

Her trembles were back, brought on in part by fatigue and another part by remembering what she'd been through.

"That's enough talk about this," Dylan said. "Time to get her out of here. Matt, Sean, I'll get the rest of the details from you later. Call me if anything new comes up. Let's get you home, Erica."

"I agree," Cam said, pulling her out of the booth.

She gave her brothers and Nicole a hug and waved at the crowd as they exited. "Thank you," she said, smiling. She was overwhelmed by the love and support the people of Destiny had shown for her tonight.

And now, Dylan and Cam were going to spend the night at her house. How long had she wanted just that? Ages. But that had been a different time and she'd been a different person. She still wanted them with all her heart, but she had a long road ahead of her to get back to normal. Normal? Would she ever be normal again? Another round of trembles took hold of her, and she would've fallen to the sidewalk if Dylan hadn't caught her in his arms.

"I've got you," he said from behind his sunglasses. "It's way past time to get you home."

* * * *

Cam unlocked the door to Erica's house and Dylan carried her inside. He turned the bed down and stood aside as Dylan lowered her to the mattress and took off her shoes.

Cam saw how exhausted she was. "Go to sleep, baby."

"We'll be right on the other side of the door," Dylan added.

Erica's eyes were wide. "Please, stay here. I don't think I can go to sleep if I'm alone. Every time I close my eyes I see the two Russians' faces."

"Of course," he said, crawling in next to her.

He turned to Dylan, wondering what he would do. Back in the car on the way to Destiny, Dylan had said he would take one step at a time. This was a step, a step to a chance at a future with Erica. Would his brother take the leap of faith now? She needed them, needed both of them. Cam knew it in his very bones.

Come on, Dylan. Stop standing there like a deer in the headlights. Let her know you care about her.

The seconds ticked by quickly. Finally, Dylan did something that surprised him. He removed his sunglasses and got into the bed on the other side of Erica.

In no time, Erica and Dylan were asleep.

Cam believed the life he'd always wanted with them might be coming true. Out of this horrible tragedy they had finally opened up to each other. He could still tell that Dylan was holding back. Why? He wasn't sure, but at least he had taken one step forward. Erica, too, had to work through her pain. However long it took for them to heal from their wounds, he would be there. He wanted a family. This was his family. He'd known Erica all his life. The time he'd spent with her these last few months had made him realize she was the one. He loved her. She was his and Dylan's forever.

* * * *

Cam looked at the clock. They'd all slept over twelve hours. Dylan and Erica were still asleep. He quietly got out of the bed. Erica stirred for a moment and then rolled over in her sleep, placing her arm around Dylan. His brother didn't stir, which was way out of character for him. It was obvious that they were all so comfortable together.

He walked out of the bedroom to the kitchen to get some coffee made. It would be quite a job to get those two to be real with each other. Whatever it took, he would do it.

Cam returned to the bedroom with three cups of coffee. Erica was awake with a big smile on her face, which made his heart swell. She looked like her old self.

"How are you, sweetheart?" he whispered, seeing Dylan was still down for the count.

"I had the most delicious dream." She giggled and then brought her hands up to her mouth.

He handed her a cup of coffee. "Tell me about it."

She shook her head. "I couldn't possibly do that."

"You can't or won't?" Dylan asked, leaning up on his elbow.

"Good morning to you, too, Mr. Strange," she said.

"It's not morning," Cam told them. "It's after seven in the evening."

"What?" Dylan's eyebrows shot up. "That can't be right. I never sleep that long. Ever."

"But you did. So did I." He smiled and grabbed Erica's hand. "I think I know why, too. Would you like some coffee, bro?"

"Thanks, Cam," his brother said, taking a cup. He placed his other arm around her shoulder, squeezing tenderly.

He'd never seen Dylan act so comfortable around anyone like he was with Erica. Still, something inside Cam told him that Dylan was holding back. Why? No clue. His brother did keep many secrets, but he wasn't about to let his foot off the pedal with him and Erica. The three of them belonged together.

Liking how Dylan was treating Erica, he thought it might be a good idea to give them a little time alone. "If you don't mind, I think I'll excuse myself to go take a shower."

"Good idea," Erica said. "I definitely need one, too, since it's been…oh my God, I haven't had a shower since Friday morning."

"That makes three of us." Dylan leaned over and gave her a kiss. "You both know I'm big on conservation."

"Not that I've ever seen," Cam told him.

"Well, it's true. I think everyone needs to do their part," Dylan said with a wink. "Water is my big issue." He jumped off the bed and held out his hand to Erica. "Let's shower together."

He loved how Dylan worked a plan. This was going better than he hoped it would. Dylan seemed to be fully on board.

Erica's cheeks brightened and she smiled. "If it means saving the planet, then I guess I better."

"Damn right," Cam said, feeling his cock harden in his jeans.

Chapter Five

When Dylan lifted her off the bed and into his arms, Erica's breath caught in her chest.

This was happening. Finally. She'd dreamed of being with the Strange brothers for years. *I want this more than anything, but will they break my heart?* Sure she'd desired this, but all that had ever happened between her and them up until now was a few teasing glances.

In the end though, the flirtations had resulted in only flirtations and nothing more. Now, the brothers were taking things to the next step, the next level. Should she? There was no doubt in her that she wanted to, wanted it with all her heart. But wasn't that what was at risk? Her heart?

If she had any chance of retreating from this promise of pleasure, she had to do it now. *Right now.*

Without a word, Dylan smiled at her. Keeping her secure in his hold, he bent down to retrieve his sunglasses.

She put her hand out to stop him. "You've got to be kidding. Don't tell me you shower with those on." Gazing into his eyes, which were the deepest chocolate brown she'd ever seen, she felt a shiver roll up her spine. "Your eyes are gorgeous, Dylan. Please put the glasses down."

For a long moment he just stared, causing her to tremble.

Is this really happening? Maybe I better pinch myself to be sure it's not a dream. "Ouch!" *It's real. It's very real.*

Cam came up behind Dylan. "What happened, baby? Everything okay?"

She thought about telling him the truth—that she was out of her mind for pinching herself—but decided that would sound ridiculous. "It was nothing. Let's just say I was checking on…on my pulse. That's it. My pulse."

"Mmm. I've never in my whole life heard of anyone getting hurt checking their pulse," Cam said.

Dylan winked at her. She could tell he saw what she'd done and likely knew why she'd done it.

Her heart skipped several beats as he placed the shades back on the nightstand. The last ounce of her hesitation vanished.

"Erica, you've put me and my brother under your spell," Cam said, brushing the hair out of her eyes.

"If it is a spell, it has taken years to invoke." She watched him nod. It had been ages of quick flirty glances and chance meetings between them that had drove her insane with desire.

Dylan carried her to the bathroom with Cam right behind. Once inside, he lowered her to her feet.

"You are so beautiful." Cam leaned over and kissed her tenderly. Her pulse quickened and her toes curled as his tongue tangled with hers.

She heard Dylan start the flow of water in her shower. *We're really going to do this.*

"Time to get you out of your clothes," Cam said, removing her top first.

He grabbed her around the waist and placed his hand at the nape of her neck, capturing her mouth once again. His lips demanded her surrender. His fingers drifted down to her bra straps, which he pulled off her shoulders. He kissed her neck as he unclasped her bra, releasing her breasts. Heat sparked in her belly, which blazed out to the rest of her body.

Cam caressed her breasts, causing her nipples to peak and throb. "Fuck, these are beautiful." His tone was lusty and awestruck at the same time.

She had no defenses left to resist, not that she wanted to. She wanted this, wanted them, wanted to drown in their pleasure.

Glancing over Cam's shoulder, she saw that Dylan had stripped. His body was a muscled machine, though the scars across his chest made her heart ache for him. Those wounds were deep. What had given them to him?

"You've finished only half the job, bro," he said, coming up next to Cam. "I'll get her out of the rest of her clothes while you get yours shucked."

Cam nodded, stepping back, making room for Dylan.

Though Dylan's body was a masterpiece of male perfection, she couldn't seem to stop staring at his eyes. Seeing him without his sunglasses made her feel special and wanted.

She glanced over at Cam. He was stark naked now, just like Dylan. She let her eyes drink in his muscles, which were tanned perfectly. When did he have time to get sun on his skin? He was always in court. But she knew he loved the outdoors more than most. Then she realized that he'd been only halfway through his two-week vacation from TBK when she'd been taken. She tensed, recalling her abduction.

"What's wrong, Erica?" Cam said.

She shook her head, not ready to say how shaken she really was. "Nothing. Just wondering why you are here?"

"Here? At your place?"

"No. Why aren't you still on leave from work?" she asked, hoping to settle her frayed nerves down. "When did you get back? Where did you go?"

"Quite the little interrogator," Dylan said with a light nod. "Watch yourself with this one, Cam."

"You know I will. I cut my time short," Cam told her. "Glad I did. If I hadn't, I wouldn't have been back to come get you with Dylan."

Again, the memory of being in that trunk flooded her mind.

"Let's not rehash past events," Dylan said, his eyes seeming to peer into her deepest secrets.

"I agree," Cam said. "There's a time to talk and a time to touch. This is touching time, don't you think?"

"Yes, it is," Dylan said with a lusty growl. He loosened her pants, which fell to her ankles, leaving Erica in only her soaked panties. He smiled when she trembled, and then helped her out of her thong.

"Damn, you're beautiful," Cam said with a tone of awe.

"Time to save the planet, sweetheart," Dylan told her, lifting her back up into his arms. He placed her in the shower and then he and Cam got in, placing her between them—Dylan behind her and Cam in the front. The warm water felt amazing. The guys grabbed sponges, soaped them up, and rubbed them against her skin. Every cleansing sweep from them ramped up the heat building inside her body. Tingles began to spread through her as Cam washed her breasts while nibbling on her neck and Dylan washed her ass while kissing her back.

As the grime of the past couple of days was washed away, she began to shiver between them.

Cam lowered his mouth to her breasts, circling her nipples with his tongue, causing them to throb and ache. His hands moved down her abdomen until his fingers were at her waist. Moaning, she arched into his mouth on her breast, seeking more of the pleasure from his tongue, lips, and teeth.

As Cam quickly washed his body, she could feel Dylan's fingers part her ass's cheeks while his tongue circled the intimate, tight spot. His licks were driving her wild, and pressure began to build inside her.

The moment Dylan's torture stopped, so that he could clean himself, Cam began licking her throbbing nipples until she was lost to a blazing need. As his tongue went lower and lower, she felt Dylan renew his attack on her backside. The warm water continued to rush over her skin but that wasn't what was making her hot. The source of her temperature spiking was the men licking her pussy and ass. Dylan held her ass and Cam fingered her pussy, using his tongue as a wicked whip on her clit.

"I want you," Cam murmured between licks.

Dylan remained quiet, though his mouth and hands on her ass ordered her into a dizzying state of desire.

She wanted them, too. God knew she wanted them. "Please. I need you. I need this." Her brain was spinning and her body was burning, both with one want—to be filled by them, to be claimed by them, to drown in pleasure until all that remained in her world was this moment, with Dylan and Cam. No Russians. No trunk. No guns. Just here. Just now. Just her and them.

The pressure grew and grew and her trembles expanded and spread out through her body. More licks. More caresses. When Dylan laved her ass with his hot tongue and Cam captured her clit between his tightening lips, her womb convulsed as her climax exploded through every cell of her body, every synapse, every nerve—everywhere.

Giving in to her need to touch them, to connect with them in that instant, she grabbed Cam's hair with her left hand and shot her right hand behind her until she could feel the top of Dylan's head.

"That's my sweet girl," Cam uttered.

She closed her eyes, relishing in the sensations shooting through her body.

Dylan licked his way up her back until he was kissing her neck. Cam's hands were back on her chest, massaging gently. With only their hands, they guided her to turn until she was facing Dylan.

"Give me your lips," he demanded, his Dom side coming through.

She parted her lips ever so slightly as he crashed into them with his own. Her toes curled and her belly flip-flopped as he deepened his kiss. She could feel Cam's hands come around her from behind until his fingertips were on her clit, once again raising her hunger back to a delirious state.

"Let's take her back to the bed," Cam said.

Dylan released her mouth. "I agree. I want to be inside her."

She wanted that, too. Needed that more than anything right now.

As they helped her out of the shower, her climatic tingles continued, and her body would not be still. She clenched her fists and chewed on her lower lip, trying to keep her head. It wasn't working. Not one bit. Dylan and Cam dried her off with a towel and then Cam lifted her up in his arms.

Dylan bent down and pulled out a condom from the pocket of his pants. "I only have one, Cam. You?"

"Left top pocket. There's one in there," Cam told him.

He bent down and got the promised package from Cam's jeans. "Perfect."

Cam carried her back into the bedroom with Dylan close behind. He lowered her onto the mattress. She watched the gorgeous, lusty men roll the rubbers down their shafts. They meant to fuck her, really fuck her. That was what she wanted. That was what she craved.

Dylan didn't wait, but crawled on top of her, leaving Cam to fist his cock. Dylan's body was like steel. Hard. Strong. She felt his cock pressing against her wet pussy as he positioned his body to grant him the best access to her most intimate flesh.

"It's been a long time." She was surprised how weak and trembling her tone was.

His smile went straight into her, coiling a new ball of want within her body.

She felt Dylan's cock pierce past the lips of her pussy and into her channel, inching ever so slowly into her body. The delicious agony expanded within her, making her warm from head to toe. Dylan's claiming of her was driving her insane. Another inch and another.

He was so big, so massive, so monstrous.

Another inch.

She fisted the sheets, feeling her breaths turn to pants and her heartbeats turn to heart skips.

Another inch.

She screamed as he hit the spot that always left her trembling.

Another inch.

Deeper.

When he was fully inside her, stretching her beyond reason, he began a slow, steady rhythm. His thrusts were dark and dangerous. She wrapped her legs around his muscled body, pulling him deeper into her sex. In and out he sent his cock. Her clit throbbed like mad and her tingles were like hot raindrops on a once-still pond. But she wasn't still. Nothing about her was still. Everything was vibrating, moving, shaking. Fingers. Toes. Skin. Lips. Inside and out, her body was alive, firing on every nerve ending. Again and again.

Suddenly, Dylan pulled out of her, leaving her wanting.

"What?" she panted out. "What's wrong?"

"Nothing," Dylan said between clenched teeth, his lust evident in every syllable. "Cam wants you, too."

But she sensed something else in him, something unspoken. Was he holding himself back for some other reason? What would that be? She told herself she was only being foolish. They were here with her. Right now. They wanted her, of that she felt certain.

Dylan kissed her, devouring her moans. He rolled off of her, and she instantly missed feeling his weight on top of her. Thankfully, Cam's body moved over her.

As Cam kissed her, she felt the warm knot of want within her begin to unravel. As she'd done with Dylan, she wrapped her legs around him, deepening their connection. When he sent his thick, long cock into her pussy, liquid poured out of her as his thrusts came hard and fast inside her. She shifted her hips, welcoming him into her body. Every one of his plunges sent her higher and higher. She went over the edge. The explosive release of pressure washed through her like a flood of hot water, sending sizzling fast pulses in her veins.

Her pussy tightened on his cock as she screamed out his name.

"Cam!"

She looked over at Dylan, who had removed the condom and was now fisting his cock like a madman. His eyes were narrowed in lust but they never left hers. This was how they shared a woman, one taking her and one watching. She felt like an exhibitionist at the moment, which mingled with her already shooting sparks, ramping up her climax even more.

Another scream and another.

"Going to come," Cam growled, his thrusts coming faster and faster.

"Please," she begged, never moving her gaze from his brother. Dylan was close, too. She reached out and cupped his balls. With her other hand, she clawed at Cam's shoulders.

"Fuck!" Dylan yelled, shooting his seed onto her arm.

Cam's body became rigid, and she could feel his cock pulsing inside her pussy.

Erica closed her eyes and tried to calm her racing pulse. She knew no matter what happened in the future, she would never forget this moment.

Chapter Six

Dylan was up on his elbow in Erica's bed. His cock was throbbing like mad. He'd wanted to thrust his dick into her sweet, wet pussy, but he couldn't.

She and Cam needed each other. His plan was working. He should've been happy about it, but he wasn't.

He looked at them, sleeping deeply, wrapped in each other arms.

Erica's lips vibrated slightly with each of her unconscious breaths, adding to his temptation to kiss her.

That couldn't be. One kiss and he wouldn't be able to keep his head, his control, or his vow. If he dared, that would send him over the edge and he would claim her as his own. But that could never be.

He did allow himself to touch her long silky hair. He felt his gut clench. How could he say good-bye to her? To Cam? To Destiny?

He'd have to do it just like he'd done the first time when he left his hometown. No words. No tears. Just leave.

He shouldn't have come back, but after all the blood he'd shed he'd needed to be with family again, to feel human again, to breathe the healing air of Northern Colorado again.

He'd been back for four years now. Two years at TBK. Eric and Scott had been thrilled to bring him on. As the Knight brothers' company had exploded exponentially, Dylan had grown too comfortable, fooling himself into a belief he might end up building a life here. But that wasn't possible. Not for him. Not with all his baggage.

Erica's eyes opened, and he pulled his hand back from her locks.

Dylan didn't want her or Cam to awaken fully. "Go back to sleep,

Erica," he whispered.

"You, too," she urged with a yawn.

He couldn't look away from her, God forgive him. Erica was not only beautiful. She was also kind and honest. Her heart was enormous, especially for those in need, whether two-legged humans or furry four-legged creatures. He was remembering when they were in high school and she spotted a little stray puppy, picked it up, took it home, fed it, and made sure it was placed in a good home.

No wonder Cam had fallen so hard for her. Cam would never understand why he wouldn't go down the path to making this fledgling relationship more permanent. No one would. Not his mom. Not his dads. Not a soul in Destiny.

His mind brought up images of his parents and the loving life they continued to enjoy. His dads and mom had grown up in Destiny, too. Pop Stephen, Papa Eddie, and Dad Albert were brothers and from the Strange family, one of the first to settle in Northern Colorado. Mom was a Blue, another longtime surname in Destiny. She was aunt to his cousins—Phoebe, Shane, and Corey—and twin to their mother, Alice. Like Dylan's sisters, Jane and Alice Blue were complete opposites. Aunt Alice was always the life of the party and full of fire. Jane, his mom, was just a little more quiet and sweet.

His family expected him to join in a plural marriage. How could he tell them that was something he just couldn't do? In the back of his mind he'd always known it, but after spending time with Erica, horizontal time, the ugly truth had crawled to the front of his consciousness. Most of his reasons were classified, so he wouldn't be able to tell them even if he wanted to, which he definitely did not. The body count was too high. Yes, he was doing his duty. Always. But the casualty of his last operation would haunt him for the rest of his life.

"What are you thinking about?" Erica scooted up the bed until she was sitting with her back to her pillow, which was now leaning against the headboard.

"So you're definitely not going to go back to sleep, I see," he told her.

"Nope. Hard to sleep." She shook her head. "Too much to process right now."

He could see it in her eyes. The pain of all that had happened to her crushed him. He wanted to kiss her, to hold her, to tell her everything was going to be okay. But he couldn't. Maybe it was selfish of him in a way, but he knew another touch would ruin him. He would forget his plan, his self-imposed mission and make love to her again. That wouldn't be good. Not one damn bit.

"Have you thought about talking to Sam about what happened?" he asked her. Though he didn't care for mumbo jumbo psychological BS, Sam O'Leary might be the only man he would ever consider going to see. He wouldn't of course. It wasn't something he could do. Sharing. Opening up. Honesty. Not part of the job. Not part of the mission. Not part of his makeup. Not one damn bit.

"Maybe," she answered. "I just don't know what I need to do. I'm a complete mess, Dylan. I have been ever since the Felix incident. After what happened with the Russians, I'm a wreck. I'm scared of my own shadow." Her voice began to crack.

Like it or not, he had to hold her. She needed him right now. The mission, *his mission*, to get Erica and Cam together as a couple, would have to wait. He grabbed her and squeezed.

"Don't worry, sweetheart. You're dealing with a ton of things. There are operatives in the Agency that haven't seen the kind of action you've dealt with. It's a lot."

"Yes, it is," Cam said, letting him know that he, too, was now awake. "You're doing great, baby. Trust me. You'll get through it."

"I hope you two are right. I just don't know." Erica leaned her head into Dylan's chest and he felt his hardened heart soften. "I want to go back to our lessons at the gun range. You will do that for me, won't you?"

"Yes, I'll do it," he said. *Time to get the mission underway.* "I think Cam should join us. Don't you? He's quite the shot as you saw in Denver."

She nodded and then he saw the subtle signs of her anxiety pop up. Her quivering lips. Her shallow breathing. Her clenched fists. He'd made a mistake mentioning Denver. It had clearly taken her back to last night in the warehouse.

"What time is it?" Cam asked, obviously sensing the change in her, too.

"Late. Nearly eleven," he told him. "We should all go back to sleep. We can hit the gun range in the morning."

"That sounds great to me," she said, her dark mood lightening. "What time?"

"Eager, are you?" He grinned and touched her cheek. "How about nine? We can grab a bite at the diner."

"Let me have my phone. I can text Scott and Eric and tell them I'm going to be in late and make sure they don't mind. I know the gun range at the house is soundproof, but I don't want to come over uninvited."

"Your phone was trashed," Cam told her.

"What about my laptop?"

"It's at TBK. The Texans have it. I think it's salvageable." Cam kissed her on the back of the neck. "I'm awake now. I have an idea we might all enjoy."

"You do?" she asked coyly, clearly warming up to what Cam was suggesting. "What about you Dylan? Are you fully awake?"

His cock sure was, already lengthening to the max. He knew he shouldn't, but he couldn't help himself. One more taste of the forbidden fruit and then he would get back on track with the steps he'd planned for them. Just one. No more.

"You tell me if I'm awake or not." He traced his fingertips down her shoulders and then took her naked breasts in his hand. God, he couldn't get enough of her. Erica was the perfect package.

"You're definitely awake," she giggled.

As he devoured her lips with his, the plan whirled in his mind.

He would hate leaving her, leaving his brother, leaving Destiny. But he must. Erica and Cam's happiness depended on it.

* * * *

Erica held the Glock in her hands. Cam and Dylan were behind her. The target silhouette of the man was thirty yards ahead in the enclosed gun range below the Knight mansion. She had the earplugs in as did both the Strange brothers. Strange? That was the right word for everything in her life now. It was Monday. She should be at work, but when she'd texted Eric and Scott the night before, they had demanded she take the week off. She wouldn't. She would go in later today. It was what she needed, though she wasn't sure if it would get her back to normal. What was normal? Nothing would be ever again.

She felt a tap on her shoulder. She turned around, keeping the pistol pointed ahead.

Cam mouthed the words "Do it."

She nodded and turned back around.

She should've shot the target by now, but she hadn't. How long had they been in the basement? An hour at least. Dylan had given her his standard gun safety instructions. She'd heard them before during their previous sessions, but he always started with them. No matter how many times he told her what was safe and what wasn't, she just couldn't seem to get used to holding a pistol in her hand. Shooting it was even harder.

Another tap on her shoulder. Again, she turned. This time it was Dylan, in his signature sunglasses. He motioned for her to put the gun down and hit the safety button that would prevent it from firing. She did, happy to be free of the thing.

He took off his earplugs and she did the same. "What's the trouble? Why aren't you shooting?"

"I don't know. It just seems weird to hold the gun. I know I'm from Destiny where most people grow up around guns and get their own at a pretty young age. I just wasn't that girl. My brothers loved the ranch, loved hunting, all of it. I'm a city girl at heart. Sure, I love the outdoors, but I'm more comfortable with a cellphone in my hand than a Glock."

"You've always been shaky with this gun," Dylan said. "Maybe we should get you a smaller one. A Saturday Night Special?"

"It's not the size of the gun that bothers me. It's what I'm supposed to do with it." She pointed to the paper target. "That's not real but it is shaped like someone that is. I'm not the kind of girl who can fire a gun at someone. I know that makes me weak. I hate that I can't." She sighed. "If I could be stronger, I think none of this would've happened. I failed Megan. I failed myself. I failed everyone." The sobs were just under the surface. She didn't want the dam to break within her. She wanted to keep her composure.

Cam put his arm around her. "Why are we here then, sweetheart? If this is too hard for you, we don't have to do this."

"I have to do this, Cam. I have to get stronger, tougher. I have to protect myself."

"I know what we need to do," Dylan said. "I know what the issue is."

"You do?" she asked, looking at him in his coat and tie. He and Cam were the most beautiful men in Destiny. And they were here. *With her.*

"I do." Dylan put his hand on her shoulder and she felt electricity roll up and down her body. "There are too many people here. You're nervous. Cam knows how to calm your nerves. He's proven that, hasn't he?"

She nodded.

"I'm a bit of a task master about this kind of thing. I think I'll leave you two alone. It'll calm your nerves, Erica. You'll see."

"Are you sure?" Cam asked, pulling her in tight. "I think you're the expert in this, not me. Maybe you should stay and I should leave."

"No way. You've got this. You've got to help her. Understand?"

Dylan didn't wait for an answer before heading to the door. "I'll see you two later. Bring the target. I want to see a bunch of bullet holes in it."

"Will do," Cam answered.

Dylan nodded and then brought his hot attention her direction. There was something odd in the way he was acting. She couldn't put her finger on it, but she wasn't ready to question him. "Okay. I'll do my best, but I'm making no promises that I'll be able to pull the trigger."

"You'll do it, Erica. You're stronger than you think. You've proven that to me again and again." With that, Dylan was gone.

"Cam, did he seem odd to you?" she asked.

"You mean more than his normal?" He shrugged. "A little. I think you're breaking through his hard shell, sweetheart. Dylan is not used to people doing that. He likes his control, not just of the situation but of himself, too. You're challenging that in him."

"I am? I don't know how I could do such a thing." To her, Dylan seemed the bastion of strength and willpower. He was quite the opposite of her.

"But you are doing it, and that's very good for both of you. Now, enough stalling. Time to fire that gun." Cam put his arm around her. "I'm going to help you with that. You say you want your power back, correct?"

"Yes. I do. More than anything."

"Then you have to fire this gun. I want you to close your eyes for me."

She obeyed.

"Good. Now, I want you to imagine that you're the best shot in all of Destiny. No one can beat your aim. Not me. Not Dylan. Not anyone. Are you picturing that for me, Erica?"

She nodded. "Yes. I am." The image her mind had dreamed up was during the paintball competition that took place annually in Destiny. It'd only been a couple of months since the last one had occurred, so it was on her mind. She wasn't about to tell him that she wasn't seeing a real gun in her hand. "I got it in my head now, Cam."

"Good job, baby." Cam squeezed her shoulders. "Now, put your earplugs in. Keep that picture in your head. Fire on the target. One shot. Just one. Take your time. Feel the metal of the trigger on your finger. Breathe. Then shoot."

"Okay. You and Dylan are more alike than you think." She put her earplugs back in, continuing to imagine the paintball game. Cam put his earplugs back in, too. She lifted the Glock in her hand. It felt lighter than before. The power of the mind, she supposed, had made it seem so. She looked at the paper man down the gun range. One bullet. Just one. That's what Cam had told her. She felt her heart racing in her chest. She closed her eyes behind the protective glasses she was wearing. In her mind, she was in Central Park by one of the dragon statues. Paintball players were all around. She loved playing that game, loved how the people of Destiny came out to support the event. It was fun and the proceeds always went to a good cause. The cause this year was for Amber's new boy's ranch that Belle, her sister, and she were going to operate on the Stone Ranch.

A tap on her shoulder again. She turned back to Cam, knowing she was taking too long. She mouthed "Sorry. I'll do it."

She turned back to the target. Okay. *I'm back in the park. I'm next to The Green Dragon.* Then it hit her. That's where the Russians had caught her and placed her in the trunk. They'd gagged her. They'd put a hood over her head. Oh God. She looked down the gun range. Standing there in paper was the one with all the ugly tats. He'd wanted to fuck her, to kill her, to rape her. And he would've, too, if it hadn't been for Cam and Dylan. They had guns. Now, she did, too. She fired at the bastard. Again and again. Emptying out the clip. Three of the shots hit the paper, creating tiny holes in the man. One in the head and two in the gut. Oh God. She felt Cam's arms come around her, helping her to let go of the gun and place it back on the ledge. She reached up and grabbed Cam's shoulders, shuddering from the experience. He held her tight and rocked her gently, kissing her hair. “It’s going to be okay, baby. I’m here.”

He was here. She needed him, needed Dylan. But how could she ask them to take such a damaged woman? It wasn’t fair to them, but heaven help her she couldn’t see herself living without them.

Chapter Seven

Cameron walked into the diner. It was still early, so the big lunch rush that normally ran a little after twelve in Destiny hadn't started. There were plenty of open booths and tables. The locals weren't strong on punching clocks or marching to anyone's drum other than their own.

He'd just left Erica back at TBK. Despite the Knight brothers telling her to take the week off, she'd *told them* she wanted to be at work. He'd agreed to leave her with them knowing she was very safe in the top floor of TBK Tower. After what had happened with Felix, Dylan had been given a huge budget to tighten the security up there. It was the safest place in all of Destiny.

Dylan was sitting in a booth talking to Jason, who was out of his sheriff's uniform. They had coffee cups in front of them but no food.

Cam stepped up to the table. "Jason, how's it going?"

"I've been better," the sheriff answered. "Your cousin Shane is back in town."

"I know. He was here Sunday morning when we got back with Erica. Where is he staying?"

"At your aunt and uncles' house. They're all there, too. Alice and Phoebe haven't been too keen on me coming around the diner ever since he got sent away."

Cam knew Jason had only been doing his job. Shane had screwed up and had been caught with a bag of drugs. The problem was Jason's testimony had been the catalyst that had gotten his cousin the most stringent sentence for a first-time offender.

"Does he plan on staying in town?" he asked.

"I don't know," Jason told him. "I'd ask Phoebe, but as you know she barely talks to me these days. My two brothers are meeting up with him sometime tonight."

The door to the diner opened and in walked Phoebe.

"Damn," Jason said under his breath. "All I have to do is think about her and she shows up."

"That's quite a talent," Dylan said.

"If things hadn't worked out the way they did between us, that would be a talent I would love to have." Jason watched as Phoebe headed straight to them. "But they didn't."

Mitchell and Lucas, Jason's brothers, had always been close to Shane. Despite their friendship, they'd been the ones to turn him over to Jason, then just a deputy, for the drug possession. All of it had ended the fledgling relationship that Phoebe and the three Wolfe brothers had had with her.

Phoebe stood at the edge of their table. "Sheriff, I have some papers I need you to look over."

"How did you know I was here?"

"Shannon told me." Her phone went off in her purse. "Excuse me." She stepped back and got her cell. "Damn. Another blocked call."

Jason's eyebrows went up. "Another?"

"Just some prankster or wrong number, I'm sure."

"I can look at your papers at my office. Bring your cell with you." Jason stood. "I need to get back to work, fellows. Alexei Markov is supposed to call me with what he's dug up on Mitrofanov."

"What about the Russians?" Cam asked, taking the seat the sheriff had just vacated.

"Niklaus is a slippery SOB, that's for sure," Dylan said.

The sheriff nodded. "Those two thugs you took out back in Denver were connected to his gang. They were on his payroll just last month. According to records at the florist where they worked, they were fired three weeks ago. I'm sure the paperwork was doctored up after you killed them. Niklaus is slick. Nothing seems to stick to that bastard. According to Alexei, Mitrofanov keeps adding to his businesses, though they're all fronts, of course."

"The Texans checked with some pals back at the Agency," Dylan informed. "They found out that the orphanage where Amber had worked was using the boys as mules to move drugs to distributors. It had Niklaus's fingerprints all over it. So far, the only records they can find shows the place was only in Sergei's name, Niklaus's dead son."

Cam looked over at Dylan. He could tell that his brother had blood in his eye for the fucker, as did he. Even though they'd never met the head of the Mitrofanov clan, Niklaus was most certainly the one who was behind Erica's abduction.

"We're not going to let the bastard get away with this, are we?" Cam asked, his frustration boiling over.

"We'll get him," Jason said. "I'll see to that. Alexei is working his contacts. Something will bubble up that we can use against the son of a bitch. On that note, I'm gone. I'll talk with you guys later."

After the sheriff left, Cam waved over Desirae, the only staff in the place. She'd moved here a while back, becoming Aunt Alice's right hand at the diner. The blonde beauty was quiet, never talking much about her past. There were plenty of Doms who would love to put a collar around her neck, but she'd only been to Phase Four a few times.

"What can I get you, Cam?" Desirae asked.

"Double meat cheeseburger, please. Onion rings. And a chocolate milk shake."

"Same old Cam," Dylan said. "You've got a stomach that is ironclad."

"So do you, Dylan Strange," Desirae teased. "I just took away your plate. New York Strip. Rare. Baked potato. Loaded. Mac and cheese. Texas toast. And now you're waiting on your banana cream pie after the new pot of coffee finishes brewing."

"Thanks for ratting me out," Dylan said from behind his shades.

"I'll remember that when I decide what to leave as a tip, Desirae."

"I see. The tip goes into the jar for the waitresses. I'm on salary. Don't punish them because I speak my mind."

"I wouldn't dream of punishing them," he said. "You? Well, that might be a different story."

Why the hell was Dylan flirting with Desirae? Cam knew his brother was into Erica. More than "into." He was completely gone on her.

"Cam, try to make him behave, will you?" Desirae didn't wait for an answer.

As she trotted off, Cam stared at his brother. "What's wrong with you?"

"Not a fucking thing," Dylan answered. "What's wrong with you?"

"Don't give me that crap. I know you. You're running again, aren't you?"

"If you're implying I'm running from something, you need to be more specific. I don't know what you're talking about."

Cam shook his head. His brother could be so frustrating. "You left the gun range this morning. Why?"

"I told you and Erica why. She was crowded by both of us. Did she fire the gun after I left or not?"

"She did, but that's not the point." Cam looked at his brother's mirrored shades and saw his own reflection staring back at him. "What is going on, Dylan? Tell me."

Dylan didn't answer. Desirae returned with a pot of coffee and a chocolate milk shake. "Your food will be ready shortly. Dylan, I'm sorry. I thought we still had banana cream pie, but we're all out. I just checked. We have apple, chocolate, and peach pie. We also have German chocolate cake and carrot cake. Would any of those do?"

"Just the coffee now, Desirae. I lost my taste for something sweet." Dylan's tone was deep and dark.

Desirae seemed to notice it, too, as she scurried off right after filling Dylan's cup.

"Speak your mind, Cam. Don't hold back."

"I will. Tell me the truth about why you left this morning."

"I told you."

"Bullshit. Don't pull your CIA crap with me, bro. I know you. I've known you my whole life. Erica sensed something different in you when you left, too. It wasn't just me. So cut the crap and come clean."

Dylan took a sip of his coffee, clearly ignoring the request.

"Fine. You don't want to tell me. Then let me tell you what I think." Cam leaned forward. "You're fucking scared. For the first time in Dylan Michael Strange's life he is feeling something, and that scares the hell out of him. Am I getting warm?"

"Go on," his brother said in his typical guarded fashion. "You're the one who wanted the microphone here, not me."

"I will go on. You think you don't deserve her. You might be right about that. No man deserves someone as wonderful as her. Our job will be to do our best to make her happy her whole life. Maybe at the end of our days we might scratch the surface of earning her love. But whether we do or not, she's in love with us. I know it. I'm in love with her. You know that. I also know you're in love with her, too."

"You use that word pretty casually, bro. It's not like a chip you can pull out of a bag any time you feel like it. That word means something." Dylan set his cup down. His tone softened. "You care for her, and yes, maybe you even love her. I hope you do. She might feel the same for you, too. Again, I pray she does. Me? I'm not part of that picture, bro. I can't be."

"Why? She needs us. Can't you feel it?"

"I'm about facts, Cam. You know that, too. What I see in front of me is a man ready to take the plunge into something more permanent. That's just not where I am. Erica deserves you, not me."

Cam realized the last words that Dylan had just spoken were the most revealing. *Erica deserves you, not me.* "What happened at the

Agency that changed you so much? You're not the same."

"Don't go there," Dylan said, his tone sharpening. "I've been out for four years now. It's in the past. Besides, I couldn't tell you anything about it. It's classified."

"But something did happen, didn't it? That's what this is about. You think Erica is beyond you. That what you bring to the table isn't going to work for her."

"For her and for you, bro. I've got more baggage than you can even dream about. I want you to be happy. Both of you. I know it's not how we grew up, but you and Erica can build a lovely family together."

"That might be true, but it isn't what I want. I don't think it's what she wants either. Dylan, we're just at the beginning of this. There's a lot of ground to still cover. Sure, we've known Erica all her life, but there's more to know, to learn, to discover. She's worth it. You just have to get over your crap. Besides, it's not just how we grew up. It's not just the kind of family we want. Erica came from the same kind of upbringing as us. She lost her parents in the plane crash. Ask her what she wants? I dare you. I bet she'll tell you that she wants to be adored and shared by more than one man."

"You can make her happy, bro. I know you can."

Cam felt for his brother. The pain he carried was buried very deep. Cam had sensed it a few times, but it was closer to the surface than ever right now. Being with Erica had to be the cause. She was impacting Dylan on every level, just like he was with her. He had to shake the crazy out of Dylan. The only way he knew how to do that was to push him.

"Suit yourself. I'm sure we could find one or two other guys to build a family with. Phong's son comes to mind. Or maybe Doc Ryder and his brothers. That would give Erica four men to be with, counting me."

Dylan's fists came down on the table, disturbing his coffee and Cam's milk shake. "Don't you fucking dare do that to me."

"I knew it. You're into her bad."

"Yes. But I can't go there."

"Don't be a chickenshit. She's hurting. Take it one step at a time. Another date. A proper date. That's all I'm asking."

"Strange men don't just date, and you know that, too, Cam."

"I sure do. But that's the deal. I can't do this alone. My whole life I knew that you and I would share a woman. I'd thought it might be Erica for some time. Now, I know she's the one. One date. Do it for me, for us? She deserves that from you at least."

"So if I don't go on a proper date, as you put it, you'll bring in another man."

He nodded, putting on his best poker face. Of course he would never bring in anyone else. Dylan was the only person he could possibly share her with.

"Fine. I'll go. You're buying though. I'm not making any promises, Cam." Dylan took off his glasses. "You make me a promise."

"Okay."

Dylan put his shades back on. "When I tell you I can't keep going down the path—and trust me, that's where I see this going—you will agree to stop pushing this and to keep caring for her."

"Okay," Cam lied. Like it or not, Dylan *was* going to get on board with pursuing Erica. He would make sure of that no matter what he had to do to achieve it. She needed them both. He knew in his gut that Dylan had the same wish as he did. A life with the woman of their dreams—Erica Coleman.

Chapter Eight

Erica stared at the monitor with her fingertips hovering above the keyboard. This was her fourth day back at work, but it still hadn't fixed things, fixed her.

Cam and Dylan had been great to her these last few days. Except for the time she spent in the TBK offices, one of them was always with her. They'd escorted her to and from work every day. Cam had spent every night with her, making love to her gently and holding her as she slept. She'd missed having Dylan there those nights, but was so grateful for Cam. Still, her mind kept snapping back to the horrors of the past, especially with the two Russians who had meant to rape her.

I've got to stop this. What's wrong with me? But she knew. Everyone in town knew. She'd been a mess after the shooting up here a few months ago. With her recent kidnapping piled on top of that, she was on the brink of going completely bonkers.

I must get a grip on myself. She tried to recall one of her mother's many mantras, but none came through yet. Instead, all she could see in the back of her mind were Humpty's and Dumpty's evil leers.

She blinked several times, bringing her focus back to the monitor. The Texans still had her computer, so she'd borrowed this one from Eric. It was about to explode with all the e-mails. Most were business but several were from staff around the country that had recently learned about her abduction.

She couldn't face those good-intentioned messages yet.

What she was chasing was a sense of normalcy. Would that ever happen again for her? She wasn't sure.

Everyone had to deal with tragedy she told herself. She and the other orphans of the plane crash of September 28, 2001, had learned that early in life. Before that awful day, she'd grown up in a loving family. She and her brothers had seen what a happy marriage could be in their mom and dads. Since they were up-by-your-bootstraps kind of men, their dads had been hard on all three of them but a little harder on her brothers. Mom had always been the mediator in the family, softening the harsh sentences that their dads had issued after some infraction by Reed and Sawyer, though Reed had been the one who seemed to be more inclined to go on a joyride or ditch school than Sawyer back then.

Erica had learned to value hard work and honesty from her dads, and about having a kind heart for those who weren't as fortunate as her from her mom. Few in the county had less than the Coleman family, but her mother had always told her that money wasn't the only thing that left people lacking.

Her dads had worked for the Stone family on their ranch and had loved it like breathing. Their orphaned sons—Emmett, Cody, and Bryant—were like brothers to her even before they lost their parents. She'd been close to Eric and Scott Knight as well, but the bond tightened when they, too, had lost their mom and dads.

It had been a carefree life before that plane had gone down.

The anniversary of that event was just four days away. The town would hold a memorial service and moment of silence in remembrance of those lost, as they did every year. And she wouldn't attend, just like the years before. She couldn't go to the cemetery and stand at her parents' grave. Being there would stir memories she wasn't ready to deal with.

She was the youngest and only girl of the orphans. She still missed her mom and dads to this day, but remembering one of her mother's lessons had helped her through her grief.

Erica, we all have choices. Every day. Every moment. We can choose to focus on the dark or on the light. I choose to walk on the sunny side of life. I hope you do, too.

The intercom buzzed, jerking her from her ride down memory lane.

She punched the button. "Yes."

"Hey, it's me." Scott Knight's voice came through the speaker. "I'm bringing up someone who wants to see you."

"Yes, Sir," she said in her best mocking tone.

"Erica, I think you'll be happy to see this person."

"Fine. Bring him up."

"See you in thirty seconds." The light went off on her phone.

Erica stood, readying for another person to look at her with sympathetic eyes. Yes, what had happened had been horrible. Yes, she wasn't over it. Yes, she was terrified of her own shadow. Yes, she still didn't feel comfortable holding the Glock, which might've given her a little sense of self-protection. Yes, she felt like she was going crazy. Yes, she kept thinking about Dylan and Cam. But no, she didn't want to think about any of it or see anyone right now.

The executive elevator opened and out came Scott followed by Sam O'Leary.

Scott smiled. "It's someone you don't mind seeing. Am I right?"

"You're right," she answered. Sam, Patrick, and Ethel O'Leary were the richest people in Destiny. Billionaires. But they were more than that to her. They were like grandparents to her and all the orphans of September 28, 2001. The O'Learys had swept in and taken care of them in every way.

She felt her insides quake. "Where are Patrick and Ethel?"

Sam came up to her and hugged her tight. "Ethel is at the courthouse hearing the land dispute between the Black Oak and Savage Ranches. Patrick is riding his Harley. Would you like to talk, kiddo?"

Sam was a semi-retired psychologist. In his seventies, his bearing was engaging and kind. He wore glasses that reminded her of what John Lennon had worn, probably because Sam had told her that he had known the musician before he'd died.

"I'm not sure I'm ready to do that," she told him.

"I'm headed back downstairs," Scott said. "I need to talk to Matt and Sean about what more they've found out about that hacker. You don't mind seeing Sam back to the lobby, Erica, do you?"

"Do I have a choice? Seems like this is an ambush to me." She grinned. "No, I don't mind."

Scott nodded. He turned and went back to the elevator. Scott and Eric were in love with Megan. The woman was amazing. The change she saw in both her bosses was remarkable. No longer did they work into the wee hours. They were out of the tower by five sharp, beelining it back to the mansion and to Megan. The sweet girl was head over heels for them, too.

That was what Erica was feeling for Dylan and Cam. But how could it work if she was so broken? It couldn't. And Dylan was holding back for some reason. They seemed to be doomed.

The elevator doors closed and she turned to Sam. "I want to talk about all my problems with you, but it's hard."

"Why don't we go sit on the sofa, sweetie." Sam gave her a kiss on the forehead. "Let me talk first. Then, if you're ready, you can, but only if you're ready. Okay?"

"Okay," she said, feeling tears begin to prick at the back of her eyes.

They sat down and Sam grabbed her hands. "Erica, you can't be so hard on yourself about this. I have no doubt that you are dealing with more than any of us can imagine. Two horrific incidents happened in less than a few months and you were at the center of them. This last one, well…I…we…" Sam's voice cracked, which was unusual for him. She looked into his eyes and saw a couple of tears fall from each eye. That was something she'd never seen in the man who had been her rock after her parents died. "I'm sorry, child." He wiped his eyes. "I'm so glad you're okay."

"I am in body, Sam, but not in mind." She bowed her head and sighed. "I don't even know who I am now. After my mom and dads passed away I was sad, but not out of control like I feel now. I'm damaged in my soul." Her own tears streamed down her cheeks, the dam now broken being in the company of one of the sweetest, wisest men she knew, a man who loved her like his own. "I hurt so badly."

He held her tight and rocked her like he'd done years ago. "It's going to get better. I promise."

"How can it?"

"You have me, Patrick, and Ethel. You have your brothers. Time is what has to pass for you to heal. One day you'll have your own family, your own children. Life will go on. You'll see."

Family? She leaned back and looked at his eyes. "How can I ask any men to take a chance on me, Sam? It's not fair to them. I'm damaged. You can see it. I know you can. I can feel it. In my bones. In every heartbeat. Every breath. I'm broken. I can't ask Dylan and Cam to fix me."

"Dylan and Cameron Strange? I knew it. They've finally moved things to the next level and gotten off the dime. Fantastic. But you're right, you can't expect that from them. You have to do the hard work, and it will be hard work, to rebuild yourself. I'm here for you, Erica. I'd like you to come to my office every day for a while. Will you do that for me?"

"I guess so." She laughed halfheartedly. "I'm nuts, aren't I, Sam?"

"Everyone in Destiny is a little nuts, kiddo. That's the way we like things here."

"Thanks, but I think you're only saying that to make me feel better."

"Am I?" He grinned. "You know what Patrick is looking for when he drives on his Harley?"

"No way," she said, unable to keep herself from smiling.

"Yes way. Dragons." Sam pulled her in tight and squeezed. "So don't be so hard on yourself. My brother is the locomotive of this crazy train, not you."

She laughed, feeling a little better.

* * * *

Erica watched Cam getting the food out of the basket that his Aunt Alice had prepared for them.

The talk with Sam earlier had put Erica's mind at ease a little. So when Cam had called asking her out on a proper date with him and Dylan, she'd said yes.

Lover's Beach was only a half mile outside of Destiny on the peninsula. The place had always been called that name, but twenty years ago it had been less beach and more mud pit. The O'Learys were responsible for getting tons of white sand trucked in to beautify the space. The whole town enjoyed family time there, but on nights like tonight—full moon, warm temperatures—only sweethearts dotted the shoreline. Tonight, it was all theirs, as no other soul was around to intrude on their perfect evening.

She sat on the giant blanket that Cam had brought for them.

"I hope you're hungry," he said with a wide grin.

"I'm famished." She sipped on the white wine. The cool sweetness tasted good on her tongue. "When do you expect Dylan to show?"

"He was meeting with Jason about what he'd learned from Markov about Niklaus. I'm sure that's about to wrap up. He'll be here sooner or later," Cam said, smiling across the blanket at her. "What do you think of our date so far, sweetheart?" He motioned to the still waters of the lake, which were reflecting the moonlight, creating a hauntingly romantic touch to the evening.

"I like this very much. And the food looks and smells wonderful."

He filled one of the plates with two pieces of Blue's Diner's most beloved combos on their menu. Fried chicken, corn on the cob, and mashed potatoes drenched in cream gravy.

"Shouldn't we wait for Dylan?"

Cam handed her the plate. "I'm sure he'll call when he's on his way. You already said you were famished. Let's eat up while it's still hot."

Her stomach rolled on its emptiness, creating a slight grumbling sound. She was hungry. "And if we eat it all up?"

"I guess he'll be out of luck, but I don't think he's in any trouble about that happening." Cam peered into the basket. "Aunt Alice sent about twenty pieces of chicken and at least a half gallon of potatoes and gravy. He might lose out on the corn, though. There are only three ears. If he hurries, he might get one. If not? Oh well."

"Cameron, let's leave him one. If you don't, I'll tell your aunt you ate his," she teased.

He reached over and touched her cheek. "Okay, sweetheart. Whatever you say. Tonight is all about you."

Heat rolled through her and she smiled. "Thank you for this."

"Enough talk. Let's eat."

"Amen," she said, before taking her first bite of the most perfect fried chicken on the planet.

After devouring a leg and a breast, two helpings of mashed potatoes and gravy, an ear of corn, and another glass of wine, Erica stretched out on the blanket and looked up into the sky. The full moon washed out many of the stars so only the brightest and closest could be seen. Dylan had still not arrived. She wondered why. What had Jason discovered about Niklaus from Alexei, the Russian who was from Bliss?

She thought about asking Cam to call Dylan but decided against it. Cam kept checking the time on his cell. He clearly was wondering what was taking his brother so long, too.

Cam finished gathering up their dishes and putting them back in the basket. He left the food out and a clean plate, knife, and fork for Dylan. "That was one of the best meals I've had in a long time."

He got on the blanket beside her, his arm and leg touching hers.

"Me, too. Alice sure knows how to cook, doesn't she? I bet if she ever put Chinese food on Blue's menu, she'd even run Hiro Phong out of business."

"Don't say that around town," Cam cautioned. "You know what happened when the diner started making burgers after Lucy's opened. That nearly started a civil war around here."

She laughed. "It was nearly as bad as the fight about what the park should be named."

"Damn. I forgot that you're in the Citizens of Tradition camp. Just being here with you I'm breaking ranks with my Destiny's Citizens League."

"Oh my." She sat up and put both her hands to her mouth in mock surprise. "So far, my peeps have kept the park's name the same. Central Park. It shall be that until the end of time," she said in the most serious condescending tone she could muster.

"We'll see about that," Cam said with a laugh. "You know I am a damn good attorney. I get paid to argue with people."

As Cam stretched out next to her on the blanket, she realized she felt better tonight then she had in two months. Now if only Dylan would show up, things would be perfect.

Chapter Nine

With his hands gripping the steering wheel like two vises, Dylan sat in his car in front of the sheriff's office.

Cam and Erica were out on Lover's Beach right now. The date. A *proper* date. That was what his brother had called it. He'd agreed to go, to take another step in a direction he knew couldn't be. Why? Because he loved his brother and he loved Erica. When he'd said it at the diner to Cam, he'd meant it, too. Now, he was late. He was supposed to meet them at seven after a conference call in Jason's office.

That call had ended at five after seven, and he'd been in the car ever since, frozen in place. The key was in the ignition, but he'd been unable to turn it to start the engine. Instead, he just sat there like a moron, torn in two directions, but doing neither.

One direction—the direction that fit into his plan for Cam and Erica's happily ever after—was to leave town instead of heading to the beach where *she* was. That was the right thing to do. Leave. Don't look back. The exit plan had been in place ever since the first day he'd come home. Call it old habits or whatever, but having several contingencies at the ready was something he felt comfortable with. It had served him well many times in some pretty close calls.

Erica was the closest of all his previous calls. He'd almost lost her to those fucking assholes in the warehouse. Almost lost her for good.

But had he gone too far, felt too much?

He took a deep breath, reining in his swirling mind. "The case. That's what I need to focus on."

Alexei had learned, though it still couldn't be proven, that Niklaus

Mitrofanov had recently received a huge influx of money from an investment back in Russia. Those funds had to be from the Knights' purchase of the shill company demanded for Erica's return. Ten million US dollars. The other forty was back in TBK's accounts, since the foreign companies they'd bought into had turned out to be legit. It might be a drop in the bucket when it came to Scott and Eric Knight's fortune, but it was money lost during Dylan's watch. He vowed to get it back, whatever it took. Going after the motherfucker was something he was chomping at the bit to do. Niklaus had set up Erica's kidnapping. Though the mobster had covered his tracks quite well, Dylan had no doubt about who his next target would be. He didn't need the Agency's sanction this time.

Thankfully, the heat was clearly off Erica, now that Niklaus had the money from her abduction. His beef wasn't with her but with Jason and the Stone brothers, though the whole town was likely a target for the murderous bastard. His eldest and favorite son had been killed in Destiny. Him talking to Kip Lunceford likely was only a fishing expedition to get intel on what weaknesses were in Jason's armor.

Keeping his emotions in check had never been difficult for him until now, until *her*. For years, he'd been drawn to her like a wolf to a lamb, but he'd resisted. Deep down he'd always known that opening up that Pandora's box would end in disaster.

A tap on the glass of his driver's side window got his attention. He turned and saw Ethel O'Leary and Gretchen Hollingsworth standing just outside his car.

Even though muffled by the glass, he could still hear Ethel. "Get out and talk to us, Dylan Michael Strange. Right now."

Refusal was not an option for him with those two apparently. He opened the door and stepped out, stretching to his full height, which placed him towering over them. Just the advantage he needed with such fearsome foes. Ethel and Gretchen were both in their seventies but they weren't to be taken lightly.

"Why aren't you over at Lover's Beach, lad?" Gretchen said in her familiar British accent.

Figured the whole town knew his business now. He was getting lax. Too lax. "What do you know about that, ladies?"

Ethel shook her head. "I'm the county judge here, young man. I know everything."

"I wouldn't doubt that." He wanted to smile, but didn't. These women already had him at a disadvantage. He wasn't about to add to that. "But you didn't answer my question, Mrs. O'Leary. Neither did, Mrs. Hollingsworth."

"Listen to the mouth on this one, Ethel." Gretchen winked. "I say you get Jason over here as fast as you can and we lock the lad up for a few days. Teach him some manners."

"Not a bad idea," Ethel teased, and then turned to him. "Dylan, I love Erica like my own. She's the sweetest, dearest girl in Destiny. She's had so much to deal with long before the shooting in the tower and her recent kidnapping. You have your parents still. She doesn't."

"But you helped her through the loss of her parents, Ethel. You, Patrick, and Sam. The whole town did. Her light returned quickly, even quicker than the guys' did."

"Don't judge the orphans, Dylan." Ethel lowered her gaze to her hands. "That kind of loss never really goes away. The world is one way one day, and then it's completely another way the next—changed for all time to come."

"But Erica did get better," he said, feeling his gut clench at the thought of Erica's suffering, both past and present. "She will again."

"Will she? You're sure about that?" Ethel shook her head. "You're a good judge of a person. You see through people's façades, don't you? So do I. Erica's had darkness inside her for a very long time. I never could get her to open up about her pain, her loss. Maybe you can. She needs to face her demons."

His heart thudded like a sledgehammer in his chest. "But what if my demons are worse? What if I'm worse? What if I make her worse?"

Gretchen grabbed his hand and squeezed. "Trust in the love you feel for her, Dylan."

Ethel reached up and put her hand on his shoulder. "Love won't fail you, and it won't fail her. Now go. Get. I'll call your mom and your Aunt Alice if you don't. That's not a threat. That's a promise."

"Pulling out the big guns, I see." Dylan leaned down and kissed both women on the cheek. He wasn't a gambler, preferring to rely on likely outcomes and probabilities. But his feelings for Erica and his loyalty to his brother weren't allowing him the clarity he so desperately needed.

"Dylan, I can see you need her as much as she needs you." Ethel stepped back and fixed her sweet gaze on him. "Please, don't fail my little Erica. Give love a chance."

I want to do that more than anything.

"I'll do my best," he told them, but inside—deep inside—he wondered if going to Cam's proper date with Erica was another step closer to utter failure and a total disaster that would leave all of them bloodied.

* * * *

Cam took a deep breath of relief as he saw Dylan's car pull up beside his. "My brother is lucky," he told Erica. They were both still on the blanket but had moved to sitting positions moments ago. "I was about to eat the rest of the mashed potatoes."

"I'm glad he came," she said softly. "I need to talk to both of you."

Cam didn't like her tone, so serious and foreboding. He didn't like it one damn bit.

Dylan walked up to them, his fucking sunglasses affixed to his face, as per normal. "Sorry, I'm late. Got held up talking to Ethel and Gretchen before I could head out here."

"I can bet what they wanted to say to you." Erica swallowed the last of her wine. "Sit. Please. I need to tell you something."

Cam saw her lips were quivering. "Baby, can't we just enjoy the evening together? You've been through way too much—"

"Stop it," she snapped. "I'm sorry. I didn't mean that to come out so harshly, but I don't want to be treated like a porcelain doll that might break anymore. I'm already broken. You treating me with kid gloves isn't helping the matter."

Her pain slammed into him like a wall. "Okay, sweetheart. We're here. Talk to us."

Dylan sat down next to her. "We are here and listening. Tell us everything."

"Everything?" She lowered her gaze to her fingertips. "I wish it was that easy, but it isn't. Not for me. It never has been."

Never has been? What did she mean by that? Erica had always been the bright light in Destiny. Her picture should've been next to the word "optimistic" in dictionaries. Well, it should've been until recently.

"Then tell us what you can, Erica." Dylan put his arm around her. "We're all ears."

"Look. You saved me. I know that. God only knows what would've happened if you hadn't come when you did. But you did come. I'm safe now. The Russian guy got what he wanted. Scott told me that ten million hasn't been recovered from what was sent on my behalf. It's over."

"It isn't over for me," Cam said, grabbing her hand and squeezing. "I want you, Erica. I want you with all my heart."

She smiled weakly. "I know you do. You're like an open book to me, Cam." She turned to Dylan. "You? Not so much. You're a mystery to me, Dylan Strange. You always have been."

"Go on," Dylan said calmly.

Cam hated how this date was turning out. Whatever it took, he'd see to it that Erica and Dylan would fall in line with what was clearly the best thing to happen for all of them. They'd found each other. Love was staring them in the face. The night was perfect. The meal was perfect. Erica was perfect. Dylan? Well, maybe not perfect but the best damn brother a man could ever ask for, a man he wanted to share the love of his life with.

Fuck!

"But even if you both feel the same about me, I can't go there with you two. Not now." She took a deep breath and then sighed, one of those sighs that reached into a man's gut like a knife, hitting vital organs. "Maybe not ever."

Cam was through playing. "Getting the cart before the horse, I'd say, Erica. You, too, Dylan. We've only begun this relationship and you two fools are done before we even get one step down the path. Yes. I called you fools. I love you, Erica Coleman, but open your eyes. I want you. This idiot wants you, too. I'm sick of this. I know you've suffered. I hate what happened to you. Hate it like I've never hated anything in my life. But it's over. You're safe. You're with us. And I, for one, am not letting you go. You need me as much as I need you. Damn it, can't you see what I see?"

"I didn't know it was tough love time, bro." Dylan shook his head. "Give her a break."

"No, Dylan. He's right. I'm pushing away the two men who mean the world to me." Erica closed her eyes. "I hate how I'm feeling. I don't want to be this way. I want to go back to the way it used to be."

"I don't," Cam told them. "Silent glances at you will never be enough for me anymore, Erica. That's all we had before. I've never been one to shy away from what I want except back then with you. The genie is out of the bottle. It's never going back in."

Cam held his breath as he waited to see Erica's reaction. He hadn't meant to spill his guts the way he had. But he couldn't let the two people he loved most in life walk away from him. A sense of relief flooded through him when Erica opened her eyes and smiled. She leaned forward, pressing her lips to his.

Chapter Ten

Erica's heart was racing as Cam deepened their kiss. His tongue tangled with hers, conveying more to her than words ever could.

Dylan feathered the back of her neck with his fingers, causing her skin to tingle.

Breaking off the kiss, she stared at Cam for a long silent pause. His eyes clawed her with hunger. Her heart was already theirs, though she knew it would be ripped apart soon. But she didn't want to think about that. In fact, she didn't want to think at all. *It's not fair to use them to quiet my gloom. They deserve better.* "Maybe we should talk about this more."

"Talk is over," Cam stated firmly. "You'll listen to my body with your body tonight."

Dylan kissed the back of her neck. "Better listen to him, baby. I've never seen him so twisted up before."

Erica trembled, realizing she'd never seen Cam like this before either. He'd been sweet and tender with her these last four days. Now his intensity was like a hot, thick cloud around him, sizzling even her skin.

"Strip," Cam demanded. "Now. This date just turned to D/s, understand?"

She nodded. It had been some time since she'd been to Phase Four, but she still knew the basic protocols. Didn't they deserve this night from her after all they'd done? Of course, they did.

"We've never had a scene with her, bro. We need to know her safe word," Dylan said calmly, letting her know he was okay with where the evening was going but wanting to keep Cam reined in.

What a turnaround in the brothers. Normally, Dylan seemed the more formidable of the two, but now it was Cam who was wildly alarming.

Cam cupped her chin. “What’s your safe word, sub?”

It sounded more like a command than a question to her. “I use the colors still. The ones that I learned in my training class at the club.”

“Good. Red. Yellow. Green.” Cam nodded, and ran his hands over her breasts. “I know what to do.”

He pinched her nipples, conveying a sting to each that shot a pulse down into her core. She felt the tingles grow inside her.

She wanted to be with them. Here. Now. Wanted it with all her heart. But tonight would be their last time together.

Regardless of Cam’s passionate pronouncements, which called to that part of her that wanted to cling to them forever, the other part, the rational part, whispered that she was drowning herself in their caresses, their kisses, only to delude herself. This was only a bandage on a wound that would never heal. The more she sank and gave herself to them, the more she was most certainly headed for the bottom of a deep, dark heartbreak that she would never survive.

“Yes?” Cam asked her directly.

That one syllable held her last free exit. If she answered “no” now, there was no doubt that Cam would not push her more. He would be furious, but he would back down. This was it. This would be her last free exit to get off the tracks of the impending crash ahead.

Unable to stop her foolish heart, she kissed him her answer. Her nerve endings turned up the heat inside her. She shivered, not from the night air, but from the tingles rolling through her body.

She turned to Dylan and kissed him, too. Back to Cam. Dylan. Kissing them until her lips were swollen and throbbing and her darkness swirled to the back of her mind, giving her a tiny, much-needed respite from her pain and her memories.

Dylan’s hands drifted down the sides of her body and Cam’s did the same down her back. She loved being between them, enveloped by their muscled bodies. This was a safe place, a place she would dream about in the nights, months, and years to come.

They lifted her up off the blanket. Cam, lost to his primal need, kicked their dishes, the food, and the basket off the blanket, creating a place for her to stretch out and enjoy their caresses.

"Put her down," Cam instructed. "I want her to strip for us."

"You're running this mission, commander." Dylan lowered her to her feet. "And doing a fucking great job of it, too, I might add. Before she does, I want to taste her lips again." He crushed his mouth to hers, slicing away the remaining hesitation inside her with his tongue. Her toes curled and her heart skipped several beats. She felt moisture pooling from her pussy.

When Dylan ended their kiss, she found it hard to catch her breath. He and Cam moved right in front of her, their Dom sides clearly switched on.

"I want to see skin, sub, and I want to see it now." Cam growled his impatience.

She grabbed the hem of her shirt and began slowly sliding it up.

Cam's eyes narrowed. "Faster."

Dylan put his hand on Cam's shoulder. "Patience, bro. Let her give us a show. We've got all night to enjoy Erica."

She swallowed down her nervousness and pulled her shirt up higher, exposing a hint of her pink lacy bra. She moved ever so slowly, hoping to tease and please them at the same time. When she finally pulled the shirt over her head, both of them lowered their gazes to her chest, their lips parting ever so slightly. They were enjoying her performance, and that thrilled her. She'd never done a striptease before, but she was actually getting into it, enjoying the seduction and power it gave her.

She relaxed her shoulders and unfastened her bra slowly. Her nipples were still throbbing from Cam's delicious pinches. She lowered the right strap off her shoulder, squeezing her arms together to make her cleavage even more prominent for Dylan and Cam. Unhurriedly, she lowered the left strap off her other shoulder until the cups of the bra drifted down her breasts. She moved her hands to them, keeping them in place over her mounds.

Dylan's wicked smile and Cam's impatient stare told her that they were both done waiting. She could feel her pulse in every part of her body, but especially on the inside of her thighs. Just looking at them made her wet. In a flash, they bolted toward her, removing the remainder of her clothes with their swift fingers, confirming to her how eager they were to consume her. She wanted to be devoured by them. Needed to be.

They lowered her to the blanket, standing over her like conquerors of old. They were giants to her in more than just their statures. They were elegant, charming, good men. Dylan missed nothing behind his shades. As he walked her to her car every day, she saw him constantly scanning the parking lot of TBK. He checked her house before he allowed her to enter. She knew she was safe when Dylan was around. He was observant of the smallest details, especially in her.

Cam, too, could see her needs, which he continually provided. These last few nights, he'd made sure she ate dinner. He'd brought her lunch at the office each day, and stayed with her and held her as she slept. She felt loved and cherished when Cam took care of her.

She watched them shed their clothes. Both pulled out protection from the pockets of their pants before tossing them to the ground. Cam also brought out a small tube of lubricant.

"You came prepared, didn't you?" Dylan said and then looked at her lustily.

Cam nodded and hit her with his hot gaze.

Dylan laughed. "I can see a *proper* date is definitely my kind of date."

Illuminated by the full moon, they looked like muscled gods.

Cam lifted her off the blanket and set her on her feet. He touched her cheek with his fingertips. "What state are you in, sub?"

"Green, Sir." She couldn't believe this was happening. Being between Cam and Dylan on Sunday night had been a dream come true. Would tonight be even better? Or would it create a hope in her that just wasn't possible? She took a deep breath, uncertainty shoving and pushing and clawing her again. "Guys, I'm…I'm…"

"She's in her head, bro," Dylan said. "You just said you were green. Did it change?" he asked in the sweetest tone she'd ever heard from him. His hand found her hair. "Yes or no?"

Nothing had changed. She wanted them. They wanted her. "No, Sir. I'm still green." But she was broken. They were solid and perfect. No matter what, she knew that tonight would have to be her last time with them. She had too much work to do. Sam had said so.

"Good. Time to make love to her pretty mouth," Cam said hungrily. "On your knees, sub. I want you to suck on my cock with all you got."

She didn't dare tell him that she'd never been too good at oral sex when it came to giving. Receiving? Sunday night had proven how good she was at that, at least with them. She lowered herself down as he'd commanded, her knees on the blanket. Right in front of her was his cock—his monstrous, massive, hard cock.

Dylan moved behind her and began stroking her hair. His tenderness was impacting her forward, which was a good thing. Thinking had gotten her in trouble. The shooting at TBK Tower a few months ago and her recent abduction had awakened the old darkness, the old pain. She'd been known as sunny, always-upbeat Erica Coleman in Destiny. Better to be with them in the here and now and not in the past, where her demons lived.

Cam placed his large hands on the side of her face, an act of dominance that pulled her from her thoughts and back into her body, where sensations were zipping like wildfire. "Make love to my dick, sub. Now."

She loved hearing the urgency and demand in his voice. "Sirs, I have to tell you that I'm not very good at this."

Cam's eyes narrowed harshly. He moved his hands to her throbbing nipples and pinched again. The stings got her attention instantly. "Don't talk about yourself that way. No negativity here, sub. Understand?"

She nodded, and his eyes softened and his hands massaged her breasts so tenderly. Her eyes brimmed with tears. Cam was proving to be more than she'd ever imagined. Tonight he'd surprised her with his sharp edge—a demanding and impatient side she'd never expected. Like his gentleness, she responded to all of him.

She placed her fingers around his thick shaft, unable to encircle all of him. She leaned forward and put the tip of her tongue on the head of his cock. The drop she discovered tasted salty and savory on her lips. This was Cam's very essence. In the oddest way it defined him.

"You're doing great, baby." Dylan, too, was startling her with his attentiveness. "Make him suffer," he said with a laugh. Dylan had always seemed to her like a man to show no mercy, but right now he was caressing her shoulders so lovingly, proving she'd been wrong.

She swirled her tongue around Cam's cock's bulbous head and slid her left hand up and down its shaft.

He groaned, and she could feel his fingers vibrating on the sides of her face. "Damn, you're better than you know, baby. Fucking fantastic."

More slickness came out of the slit of his cock, and she relished every drop. She cradled his heavy balls in her right hand, squeezing ever so slightly.

Another moan from Cam urged her forward. She swallowed the head of his cock, which pulsed in her mouth. She swirled her tongue around the head, as Dylan moved lower, kissing up and down her back. Cam's hands threaded through her locks. She squeezed her thighs together as the pressure began to rise within her. She'd never cared for giving oral sex before, until now. With Cam's fingertips caressing her hair and his cock in her mouth, she wanted more than anything to please him. With Dylan's lips dancing on her back, she craved even more. She needed them to fill her, to claim her, to make her forget everything.

She sucked hard on Cam's cock until her cheeks hollowed out.

"Fuck, that feels good." His hand was at the back of her head, pulling her in more. "Make love to my cock with those pretty lips, sub."

This felt so right. Her body was on fire in this moment with them. Oral sex had always been just a task, a means to an end. But it wasn't now. Not with Cam and Dylan.

"You've got to feel her mouth on you," Cam told Dylan.

"Damn right I do."

Though her eyes were closed, she was aware of Dylan moving next to Cam, but she was aware of so much more and all of it primal. She opened her eyes, drinking in the moment. The full moon above lit Cam and Dylan's male frames perfectly. She felt Dylan's cock on her cheek, letting her know the mercy she'd seen in him was gone.

"Suck me," Dylan ordered.

She looked up, keeping Cam's cock in her mouth. "You heard him, baby. Give him a sample of your sweet mouth." There was a delicious dominance in every syllable from both of them that reached into her and seared her heart to them.

When she released Cam's dick, the desperate groan that fell from his mouth made her smile. She kept her hand on his balls but moved her other hand to Dylan's shaft.

"That's it, sweetheart." Dylan's urgent tone sent a delicious tremble through her. "Tighten those lips around me."

"Yes, Sir." She licked the tip of his cock, finding a pearly, tangy drop.

As she swallowed more of his thick shaft, Dylan buried his hands in her hair. She squeezed Cam's balls and took in more of Dylan's cock. They were both so big. Massive. She groaned as Dylan thrust lightly in and out of her mouth, sending another inch deeper down her throat. Sucking on his dick, she tried to take more of him, but she'd only taken half of his length into her mouth.

Another inch, and she moaned into his cock.

"Fuck, baby, you're were just conning us about your oral skills," Dylan said with deep, heavy breaths.

Cam chimed in, "I told you. That's a killer mouth she has."

She loved hearing their praise. She moved her hands from Cam's balls to his shaft and began pumping him.

"That's it, sub," Cam said. "Make love to my dick with your fingers."

Dylan began pulling in and out of her mouth, claiming her with every white-hot inch.

She could feel the pulse of his cock on her lips. The head of his cock tickled the back of her throat.

"You want my cum, don't you?" Dylan growled, lost to his lust. "That's what I want, too, baby. I want to shoot my seed down your throat and drown you. But not just yet."

Not really listening and only feeling this enticing moment, "Mmm" was the only thing she could respond to him. She increased her tempo, her mouth around Dylan's cock and her hand on Cam's.

"Fuck, Erica." Cam's breath sawed in and out from deep within his chest. "That feels so good. Slow down. We don't want to come this way."

As much as she wanted to obey him, she couldn't. Her old doubt crawled out of the shadows. They'd done so much for her already. She shouldn't ask them for more. So, she continued sucking and pumping them, ignoring Cam's command.

"Going to come." Dylan's admission only added to her desire to please him and Cam. She sucked on his cock as hard as she could. He pulled her head into him tighter, making her take another blazing inch. His dick jerked in her mouth and his seed shot out of him, coating her tongue. His essence went down her throat and into her.

"Fuuuck!" Cam wrapped his hand over her hand that was on his pulsing cock.

In a flash, she released Dylan's dick and swallowed Cam's cock just in time to drink down every delicious salty drop.

She removed her mouth from Cam and her hands from him and Dylan. Looking up at them, a tremble rolled through her seeing their faces flooded with a mix of satisfaction and disappointment.

Dylan's fingers traced her jawline. "Don't think we're through with you yet, Erica. We're not."

"Definitely, not," Cam said firmly. "You've been bad. Very bad."

Her jaw dropped. "But you both just came."

Cam bent down and brushed the hair out of her face. "We'll come again, sub. With our dicks inside you."

"I thought guys didn't come more than once in a night."

"We're not that old, Erica." Dylan laughed. "And we're not normal guys either."

That's for sure.

Cam stood up, pulling her to her feet. "We've drifted from D/s. No more." His gaze was hot, making her very warm. "Understand, sub?" Cam was back in Dom mode and right now, she couldn't refuse him anything.

"Yes, Sir."

His lips curled up ever so slightly but his eyes were fierce. "I'm going to feel your ass around my cock."

"And I'm going to fuck your pussy," Dylan added.

Even though she knew this was a bad mistake, a very bad mistake, she couldn't help herself. She wanted to feel them inside her body, their cocks filling every inch of her.

"But first, you have to be spanked for disobeying me," Cam told her.

"She's sorry, bro," Dylan said. "Can't you see it in her eyes?"

"Maybe so, but what kind of Doms would we be if we let her get away with that kind of behavior." Cam cupped her chin. "She's tougher than she knows."

She didn't feel tough at all.

Dylan kissed her shoulder. "I know she is."

"Color?" Cam asked.

"Green."

"Bend over and grab your ankles, sub," he commanded.

Oh God. She obeyed.

"Ten slaps to this gorgeous ass. That's what we're going to give you." Cam rubbed her ass cheeks with his rough hands, which caused gooseflesh to pop up on her skin and her clit to begin to tingle. "Five from Dylan, and then five from me. I want you to count them aloud. Got it?"

"Got it, Sir."

They shifted around her, Cam in front with his hands on her back, steadying her, and Dylan behind about to begin their lusty punishment.

"Ready?" Dylan's tone was pure animal and sent a shiver up and down her spine.

"Yes, Sir."

His open hand landed on her left ass cheek, delivering an instant burning bite.

"One, Sirs," she said, feeling fresh tears pricking at her eyes.

Slap. This time his hand hit her right cheek with an equally delicious sting.

"Two, Sirs."

Slap. Right side again and more burn.

"Three, Sirs." She could feel liquid dripping down her thighs as her pussy began to clench and her clit began to throb.

Slap. Left side. Hot. Searing. Wonderful.

"Four, Sirs."

The last of Dylan's spanks landed in the center of her ass, hitting both cheeks. She could imagine he'd left his handprint on her.

"Five, Sirs," she choked out as her body began to sizzle wickedly. She needed them inside her. Five more spanks. Cam's spanks. Then they would fill her, release the building pressure within her.

Cam and Dylan changed positions. Even the way they were now, she could see them put on the protection. They meant to fuck her, and she needed them inside her in the worst way.

"You're mine, Erica," Cam stated authoritatively. "You're mine and Dylan's. You both will understand that if it takes me all night to get that through to you."

The intensity in his tone washed through her. *No. It's not fair to you. I'm broken. I'm damaged.*

Cam rained down his slaps on her ass, one after another, each adding an exclamation point to his earlier statements. The dam burst inside her. She blinked, tilting her head a bit until she could see the tops of her toes were wet from her tears. His words swirled in her head, over and over. *You're mine and Dylan's.*

Dylan lifted her up into his arms. She wrapped her arms and legs around him, holding on with all her might. The friction of his hard cock pressing on her pussy drove her mad with desire. Cam began applying lubricant to her ass. They were going to fuck her together. Simultaneously. That had never happened to her before with anyone. She'd dreamed of this moment for years, being between the Strange brothers, giving all of herself fully to them.

Continuing to slick up her ass, Cam reached around her, pressing on her clit. She groaned into Dylan's chest.

"You want us, don't you, baby?" Dylan kissed her forehead.

"Yes, Sir. I do." The truth. The absolute truth. The pressure was overwhelming. She needed relief.

"She's going to get us, too," Cam said hungrily behind her. His fingers shot into her ass, stretching her for his cock.

Her lips vibrated and she licked at Dylan's nipples and clawed at his neck. She could feel her toes curling and uncurling, her pussy clenching and unclenching. Need, never-ending need, swamped every fiber of her being.

She felt Cam's cockhead at her anus. "Please, Sirs. Take me."

"That's what I like to hear from those pretty lips," Cam said in a low tone. "Sweet begging." He thrust his dick into her, between her still-burning ass cheeks. The stretch was intense and took away her breath for a moment.

As if she was weightless, Dylan positioned her until the tip of his cock was right at her pussy. He sent the thick monster into her body, claiming all of her with a single powerful thrust.

She screamed into the full moon as they filled her pussy and ass with their cocks. Their plunges in and out of her body sent her over the edge, and the immense pressure that had been building from the very moment she'd stepped onto the blanket exploded into a blast of sensations that ripped through her body. Wetness poured out of her as she writhed between them. They were holding her. They were in control.

Dylan's body stiffened and he moaned. She could feel his cock pulsing inside her pussy, which clenched on his shaft again and again.

Cam sent his dick deep in her ass in one final thrust and shouted, "Yes!"

She tightened as hard she could on him and Dylan, relishing in the feel of them inside her body. They kissed her while her body vibrated like a live wire and squeezed her between them. Gently, they lowered her back to the blanket, Dylan lying next to her in front and Cam behind. More kisses. More tingles, though they were slowly beginning to subside.

The darkness was gone, pushed back by the pleasure they'd given her. *Maybe I could be the woman they deserve. Maybe I could have the dream of a life with them.*

Dylan sat up. "That was quite a picnic." He grabbed up her clothes. "I'll help you, baby."

"It is getting a little chilly," she said.

Cam lifted her to her feet. She was glad, since standing on her own would be difficult. If Cam hadn't been steadying her with his arm around her shoulder, she would have certainly fallen back to the blanket. This night had left her completely spent and satisfied.

Dylan held her panties. "I think I'll keep these." He winked and knelt down in front of her with her slacks. "Lift your leg for me."

She did, and he helped her get her pants on. He stood up and put her bra back on her. Her head was spinning. She was a little dizzy still. What a night.

Dylan stood up. “Almost done.” He lifted her top and brought it down over her head.

The moon disappeared. Dylan and Cam disappeared. Her sight was gone.

She was back in the park, the Russians grabbing her. She was helpless as they placed the hood over her head and shoved her into the trunk. Lost to her terror, she felt another memory, an ancient memory, clawing its way to the surface out of her soul. She’d buried it there when she was just a teenager. Her bones chilled as the face of the man appeared in front of her—the one who inhabited all her nightmares.

She screamed at the demon inside her. “No! Don’t touch me!”

Panicking, she fought with the shirt, pulling it down until her sight finally returned.

Dylan stepped back, raising his hands to the sky. “I tried, Cam. You know I did. It just didn’t work.” He grabbed his clothes and walked away.

What had she done? Her broken mind was going to cost her Dylan. She had to stop him, to explain to him how troubled she really was. She couldn’t let him think she was afraid of him.

“Dylan, please wait,” she called to him.

He stopped but didn’t turn around.

Say something. Anything. What?

Silence had been her constant companion for so long, and once again words remained behind her quivering lips.

Erica burst into tears as she watched him walk to his car.

Chapter Eleven

Cam held Erica, who was sobbing so hard it was crushing his heart.

Dylan was gone.

He wasn't sure what had happened when they were dressing her. Everything had been going the way he wanted up until then. Dylan was on board. Erica was surrendering with every shiver. He could see both of them coming around. The future had never looked brighter to him. But something had happened to Erica. What? Dylan had vanished. He couldn't really blame him. He was the one who'd been dressing her when she'd gone out of her head.

He'd pushed her too hard. Dylan, too. This was his fault alone. He wanted to go get his brother back, make him stay. But Erica was a mess. Maybe she needed to cry out whatever weight she was carrying. Maybe Dylan was right to leave. He just didn't know.

Cam held her until her sobs turned to whimpers. She was clothed. He was still naked. He didn't care. He wanted her trust, wanted her to tell him what had shaken her so hard. He had to know. Was it the abduction? The shooting at TBK? She was strong. Very strong. This just didn't seem like her.

"I'm o–okay, now," she whispered. "I'm sorry."

"You have nothing to be sorry about, sweetheart." Cam cradled her chin, watching her quivering lips. "Talk to me. What happened?"

The woman he loved was hurting, and he didn't know how to fix it. He'd never felt so helpless before in his life.

* * * *

Erica's heart began to settle, though only a little. The memory of that awful night sank back into its dark place in her psyche, waiting for the next time to strike. "Cam, I'm so sorry about this. I don't know what came over me."

He shook his head. "That's not true, Erica. You do know. I want you to open up to me. Please. I want to help you."

"No one can help me," she told him. "I'm the one who has to work through this. I'm going to see Sam. I'll talk to him." But could she? Back when the monster had taken her virginity, she'd kept silent. Even today, the secret was hers alone. She had her reasons.

"Was this about me demanding we go D/s tonight?" His expression of guilt flattened her.

"No," she said, touching the side of his face, feeling his five-o'clock shadow, which tickled her fingertips. "I loved every bit of it, Cam. You and Dylan are the most amazing men I've ever known." Her heart sunk, looking at the empty spot where Dylan's car had just been. He and Cam had misread her reaction as something else, a rejection of them.

"If you care for me, Erica, then trust me. Tell me what happened to you tonight." Even now, there was a hint of demand in his voice, though his overwhelming notes were concern and gentleness.

She sighed. "I'll tell you as much as I can, okay?"

"Yes. That would please me very much, baby. I want to help you through this pain, whatever it is."

Erica leaned in and kissed him. "I know you do. That means the world to me." She looked into his eyes and felt her heart break. It was time to tell someone. After all these years, she must. "I was raped, Cam."

His jaw dropped and his face darkened. Thankfully, he remained silent. If he had said something, anything, no matter how kind or sincere, she couldn't have said more. Somehow, Cam knew that. She continued recounting that horrible night.

"After my parents died, we moved in with the O'Learys. I was the only girl and the youngest. The whole town embraced us, trying to ease the loss. I felt the love and it pulled me from my grief some. I wanted the boys to feel better, too. So began my cheery side. I made it my goal to help my brothers and the other boys get better. I'm a fixer. Have been ever since." She closed her eyes as the memories flooded into her mind. "Things rocked along for a while. The boys got better. I got better. Then my senior year in high school began. It was exciting and wonderful. After I turned eighteen, I concentrated on what I wanted to do with my life. Do you remember how I was back then?"

"I do," he said softly, stroking her hair. "Dylan and I were smitten by you even then, though we were already in college."

"I was raped at school, not by a student but by a teacher."

The veins in Cam's neck popped out, evidence to her that what she was telling him was enraging him. *I should stop. He's heard enough.* But she couldn't. She'd bottled up her memories for so long, and now that they were out in the open, they would not go back down.

"Go on," he told her.

"He was a beloved teacher." Her eyes were swollen from all the tears. She was all cried out. "Mr. Boyd."

"The band director," Cam said through clenched teeth.

Erica nodded. She'd been so excited to make first chair in flutes her senior year. "That's him. Or was."

"Cancer. I remember. Motherfucker deserved so much worse."

"Whenever he asked students to stay after class to help him put away instruments, I was always happy to do it. I never thought he was dangerous." He'd been her favorite teacher before that horrible day.

"No one knew about that asshole."

"I know. After he took my virginity, I ran back to the O'Learys and went to the bathroom before anyone spotted me. I jumped in the shower and scrubbed my skin, crying the whole time, praying for the nightmare to end. It didn't."

"I collected money for that dick's medical bills. Fuck."

She remembered. It had been so hard to watch the citizens of Destiny support the man who had raped her. "We all did. The whole town. I'd just mustered the courage to confess to my brothers what had happened when Boyd told the school that he had lung cancer. After that, I just couldn't tell."

"Goddamn motherfucker."

"I should've seen the signs, Cam. I shouldn't have gone into the room alone with him."

"How could you know?"

She shrugged. "I know you're right, but whenever I go back to that night in my mind, I relive the horror over and over. I still blame myself for being so foolish and not seeing the signs in Mr. Boyd. The secret was mine alone. I was able to shove it deep down inside me. Tuck it away from the light of day. Put on the happy face again for my brothers and the other boys." She shook her head. "I couldn't tell anyone. If my mom had been alive, I know I would've told her. But she wasn't. I trust the O'Learys with everything now, but back then, after my parents died, I felt like I owed it to them to be the sunny little orphan they'd taken in. Boyd died and time passed. I haven't been able to bring myself to visit my parents' graves because he is buried there too. I've missed the memorial service for them every year because I can't stand to look at his headstone. I'd kept the secret for so long, I just never could bring myself to tell them. After the shooting at the tower and after my abduction by the Russians, my memories of Boyd and the equipment room wouldn't remain still. When Dylan put my shirt over my head, it reminded me again of the hood the kidnappers had put on me. That's why I screamed. But it was more than that. The tower shooting, the abduction, the equipment room…I feel completely out of control, unable to protect myself. That's why I want to learn self-defense. That's why I wanted to go back to the gun range."

He pulled her in tight and squeezed. "I'm here for you. I won't let you go."

"I've never told anyone any of this until now. Until you."

"You can trust me, baby."

These last few days had proven that to her. "What about Dylan?"

"Don't give up on him, sweetheart. Dylan thinks he's not good enough for you." Cam kissed her on the cheek. "He's confused."

"Just like me. He's more than good enough. Let's go find him. I need to explain to him what happened."

Erica helped Cam pack up the picnic supplies, more hopeful then she'd been in years. With Cam and Dylan by her sides, she knew she could handle anything.

Chapter Twelve

Cam stood at the corner of East and North Streets with Erica, feeling his gut tighten. They'd been looking for Dylan everywhere. His house on MacDavish Lane. Phase Four. Blue's Diner. Phong's. Lucy's Burgers. Even TBK, which was deserted due to the late hour.

No Dylan anywhere.

"Where can he be?" Erica shook her head, clearly frustrated by the lack of results in their search.

He was frustrated, too. "I'm not sure. My brother was always the best at hide-and-seek when we were kids. He probably just needs some space."

"But I have to tell him that it wasn't him that had messed with my head and caused me to freak out. It was me. My crap." Erica pointed to the Swanson County Jailhouse, which had Sheriff Jason Wolfe's office inside. "The light is on, Cam. Maybe Dylan went back to talk to Jason."

"I bet you're right. Let's go see." He prayed that his brother was inside. Once Dylan heard Erica's story, Cam believed things would tilt in the direction they should. Erica belonged with him and Dylan. Cam had no doubt about that. After hearing her horrific story of the creep who had raped her at school, all he wanted to do was hold her and make the rest of her life nothing but happiness. Erica was strong. God, how had she carried such a load for so long? Once Dylan knew the truth, the three of them could begin building a future together.

As he and Erica walked into the office, Shannon Day, Jason's eccentric dispatcher, greeted them with a broad smile. "Seems like we have a crowd here tonight."

It was odd to see Shannon here at this hour, but the sixty-year-old woman, like most in Destiny, followed her own rules, and that included her work schedule. The bright blue wig she wore tonight was one of many colored wigs she owned. “Jason isn’t alone?”

“Nope. Go right in. I’m sure he’d be happy to see a friendly face right now.”

Cam didn’t like the sound of that. Not one fucking bit. They opened the door and walked into Jason’s office. Jason wasn’t alone, but his guests didn’t include Dylan.

A bald, heavyset man sat in the chair in front of Jason’s desk. The guy wore a dark suit and had an unlit cigar in his mouth. Cam guessed him to be in his early sixties. Two men stood behind him, also in dark suits. They had tats on the sides of their necks. They looked like some kind of insignia.

“Where’s your brother?” Jason asked Cam, his face tight.

“We thought he might be with you,” Erica blurted. “We don’t know where he is.”

The creepy fellow in the chair rose and reached for Erica’s hand. “Perhaps I can be of service to you, *dushka*.”

The Russian accent chilled Cam’s bones, causing him to step between the man and the woman of his dreams. “Who are you?”

“Your forgiveness, sir. I did not know this lovely lady was taken.” Slime rolled from every syllable the bastard uttered. “But you are correct. I did not give you my name. That is why I am here with the good sheriff. I am a new resident of Destiny, Colorado. I should mind my manners.” The man held out his hand. “My name is Niklaus Borisovich Mitrofanov. And you are?”

He grabbed the man who was most certainly responsible for Erica’s abduction by the collar. “You fucking sonofabitch. I should kill you.”

The men behind him reached in their jackets for what had to be pistols. Cam didn’t have time to get his Glock from the holster under his coat. Dylan always told him he was too rash and reacted too fast without thinking. This was one of those times. He should've pulled out his gun first and aimed it between the motherfucker's eyeballs.

"Mitrofanov, I'm the law here." Jason's gun was drawn. He'd jumped to his feet the second Cam had grabbed the Russian kingpin. "Your two bozos pull out weapons, and you won't like what happens next."

"They are a bit overprotective, Sheriff. You must forgive my nephews." Niklaus held up his hand, motioning for his two thugs to stand down. "I'm not sure why you're so angry with me, young man. I came to introduce myself to Sheriff Wolfe. That's all. I'm certain there has been a mix-up of some kind. If you will kindly remove your hands from my coat, we can all sit down and work this out. What do you say?"

Cam glared at Mitrofanov. "Only this, asshole. Keep. Away. From. Erica." He removed his hands from the man's collar.

"Who is Erica?" The mocking amusement in the bastard's eyes could not be missed.

"I am," she said, coming around Cam. "Do you know where Dylan Strange is, Mr. Mitrofanov?"

Placing his arm around her protectively, Cam hadn't thought about that possibility.

What if Niklaus was responsible for Dylan's disappearance? Sure, his brother had left on his own accord back at Lover's Beach, but what if he'd intercepted Mitrofanov and his two tatted nephews. Was Dylan in a trunk now, like Erica had been? The odds were slim that anyone would get the jump on his brother. But Cam couldn't rule out that possibility. Dylan had been upset when he'd left. Even with all his training, Dylan might've been off his game.

"I'm sorry, miss. I don't know this Mr. Strange fellow." Niklaus pulled out his unlit cigar and twirled it between his fat thumb and forefinger. "My offer stands of trying to help you, should you choose. Shall we all sit down and get the facts on the table?"

"The fact is, Mitrofanov, you are a suspect in Miss Coleman's recent abduction." Jason set his gun on his desk, but it was still only a fraction of an inch from his hand.

The false look of shock on the bastard's face made Cam's jaw tighten. "When did this crime happen, Sheriff?"

"You fucking know that." Cam poked Mitrofanov in the chest. "If you did anything to my brother, you will have me to deal with. Got it?"

"Do you gentlemen have any proof of the accusations you are hurling at me?"

Jason sneered. "Not yet, but we will."

Cam pulled Erica in tight and led her out the door, away from the monster who was taking up residence in their hometown.

* * * *

Erica sat across from Cam in one of the booths at Blue's Diner, the only restaurant in Destiny that was open until midnight. Midnight? It was fast approaching and they still didn't have a clue where Dylan was. Her heart was racing. What if that Russian in Jason's office had done something to him? She'd screamed and Dylan had left. Had she caused him to be caught by the mobster's thugs?

"Have you tried to call him?" she asked Cam.

"No, I haven't. When Dylan doesn't want to be found, it doesn't matter what you do. He won't answer."

"Please, Cam. Try."

Though he knew it would be fruitless, Cam reached into his coat and frowned. Then he patted his pockets. "I must've left my cell at the beach or in my car."

"I'll try him," she said, pulling out her cell. It rang and rang. Then Dylan's voice mail message came on, filling her with dread. "No answer. We've got to do something, Cam. Where haven't we looked? Maybe we should go to Dylan's house again?"

"Honey, I'm sure he's not there. I'm sure he's fine. You and I both know his background. He's got the best training the CIA can dish out."

"You know that for sure," she said. "How? He never talks about the past with anyone. Does he with you?"

Cam shook his head. "I don't think he's allowed to. You know the government and their secrets."

"I suppose you're right. Dylan has a ton of secrets of his own, I'm guessing."

"You're right about that." Cam reached across the table and grabbed her hands. "He needs you, Erica, as much as you need him. I know it. We'll find him."

She wanted to believe that, wanted to with all her heart. "The CIA. Wait. Matt and Sean worked for the CIA. I remember Dylan saying that before they moved here from Texas. They all worked together. Maybe they can help us find him?"

"Beautiful and smart. Quite the package."

She pulled out her cell and dialed the Texans. "I'll have them meet us at TBK Tower, so they can use the computers there."

"Great idea."

Two minutes later, they were out the door and headed for TBK. Erica hoped the Texans were as good as everyone said they were. She had to get to Dylan and explain what happened or the three of them didn't have a chance at happiness.

* * * *

Dylan sat on the bed of the motel room he'd rented for the night. He'd driven into Goodnight, Colorado, a town about an hour outside of Destiny, knowing if he stayed home, Cam would have eventually found him. He knew his brother was beyond angry with him for walking out on Erica.

He stared at the bottle of whiskey on the nightstand. The amber liquid inside tempted him. Sure, it was a crutch, but it was a familiar crutch.

He'd picked up the bottle on his drive here from Lover's Beach where he'd left *her.*

Erica had screamed and his world had crumbled. Why had he let Cam talk him into taking another step down the path that he knew led to nowhere? *Because I couldn't stop thinking about her.*

He grabbed the liquor bottle. Killing came easy to him. He was damn good at it. Some at the Agency even said the best. It had been years since he'd bought whiskey. The last time he'd considered drinking after a mission had been four years ago. He hadn't, but instead returned to Destiny to try to get his head on straight. It had worked for a while. Now his head wasn't on straight and the bottle was calling to him.

He set it back down on the nightstand—its contents undisturbed—next to his sunglasses. Even though the only light in the dark room was coming through the cheap mini blinds, he put the shades on.

Where to go from here?

Not back to Destiny. He would only fuck up the good thing that was happening between Cam and Erica. TBK had been the best job of his life, though his old boss at the Agency had called it a high-class security guard detail after he'd taken the position two years ago. He'd never minded the ridicule, glad to be back home, close to his brother. But he could not go back. Ever. He'd made Erica scream. That sound continued to echo in his ears.

His gut twisted into a knot. He left the bed and went to the bathroom, which had the only glass in the room. He leaned against the sink and looked at his reflection, dimly lit from the outside light. He saw a monster staring back at him, holding an empty glass instead of a gun. Still, the man in the mirror was a killer.

There was only one thing he could do now, though he'd been running from it for four years. One person who had never given up on him, wanting him to return to the life he'd left.

He walked back to the bed and pulled his cell out of his jacket.

Staring at the whiskey bottle, he punched in a number at the Agency with his thumb. It was time to accept the truth.

He brought death. Erica was life itself. He was no good for her.

"Strange, is that you?" his old boss asked.

"Yes, Black." Dylan set the glass down by the unopened bottle. "It's me."

* * * *

Erica stood behind Matt, staring at his monitor. Cam was behind Sean, who was typing on his keyboard. She was so anxious. They hadn't found anything that pointed to where Dylan might be, so her worry continued to expand inside her.

"He's good," Matt said. "Always was."

"What do you mean?" she asked him.

"When an agent of Dylan's caliber doesn't want to be found, they can't be found no matter how hard you look."

"Don't tell her that," Cam barked. "She's already a bundle of nerves."

"Not a single hit on his credit cards," Sean said.

"What about his cell?" she asked them. "Anything?"

Matt shook his head. "Dylan is likely using a burner phone."

She had no idea what that was, but did know that it meant they were right back where they started. This search was going nowhere.

Her heart clanged in her chest like a warning bell. She still was picturing Dylan inside a trunk, bound and gagged as she'd been. She hoped he'd vanished from Destiny of his own accord, like the Texans were suggesting, even if that meant he'd been the one to run away when she'd freaked out at the beach.

This is all my fault.

"I've got an idea," Sean said. "It's time to call in the big guns."

Matt turned to him. "Black?"

"Yep. He's got the resources that can really step up our search."

Sean brought out his cell. "Besides, he's fond of Dylan. You remember."

"How could I forget?" Matt nodded. "Dylan was the best at the Agency. Everyone knew that."

"Does Black work at the CIA?" Cam asked.

"Yep, though I'm sure that's not his real name," Matt answered.

"Black, this is McCabe," Sean spoke into his phone. "Yes, sir. The reason I'm calling is we're looking for Strange. We think he might be in trouble. He did?"

Erica wished she could hear both sides of the conversation. She held her breath as Sean continued talking to the man on the other end of the call.

Sean took out a pen and wrote down some information.

A clue? Would it lead to Dylan? She prayed it would.

"Thank you, sir. We'll handle it from here." Sean clicked the phone off. "Dylan is in Goodnight at a motel."

* * * *

Dylan looked up at the ceiling, his sunglasses still on. Sleep wasn't coming tonight, not without Jack Daniel's, which was on the nightstand with every ounce still intact. Black was supposed to call him in the morning about his reassignment. His old boss had told him that some strings would have to be pulled and some favors would have to be called in to get Dylan reinstated. Black was ready to do whatever necessary to make that happen.

What if the brass at the Agency didn't let Black reinstate him? What then? He had no clue.

He heard a car pull up to one of the parking spaces outside his room's door. He sat up and brought out his gun. Old habits died hard. Whoever was outside had nothing to do with him. He was a ghost again. He knew Black would succeed. Tomorrow he would be back at the Agency.

Footsteps.

He aimed the gun at the door.

Three hard knocks got him to his feet and into the darkest corner, his back to the wall. He crouched down.

"Dylan, it's me." His brother's voice was unmistakable. "Let us in."

Us?

Had Cam brought Erica with him after what had happened at Lover's Beach? She'd screamed because of him. What the hell was Cam thinking? How had they found him?

Screams were something Dylan had heard many times, but that one, the one from her gorgeous lips, had completely flattened him.

"Please, Dylan," Erica's voice came through, reaching into him, breaking his heart. "Please let us in."

Do the right thing, Agent. Don't answer her. Black is calling tomorrow. She and Cam have a chance at a real life, a happy life, if I can keep my mouth shut.

"Cut the crap, Dylan," Cam said. "We know you're in there."

It took all his strength and determination to remain silent. They had to leave eventually. When they did, he would crack open the whiskey bottle and drown away his agony.

The next knocks he heard came from her delicate hands. "I need to talk to you. Please. Open the door."

Hearing Erica's sweet plea caused his willpower to melt into a puddle. With his sunglasses still on, he holstered his gun and walked to the door. Taking a deep breath, he opened it.

She rushed in and wrapped her arms around him. "You're safe. Thank God. Even after Sean told me about your call to Black, I wasn't sure we'd find you."

Black had given up his location? Why? That would be a question for tomorrow.

He couldn't help himself, pulling her in tight to him. "I didn't expect you to come looking. Not after what happened."

She looked up at him, her eyes glistening with tears. "This is all my fault, Dylan. I'm the one to blame. I'm so sorry."

He cupped her chin. "Sweetheart, you have nothing to be sorry for."

"No, she doesn't," Cam said. "But you left before you could find out why she reacted the way she did."

She needed to understand. He had to make her understand. "I had to leave. I'm the cause of this." He turned to Cam. His brother needed to understand, too. "I told you I would fuck this up. She needs you. You need each other. You can build a life together. A happy life. I'm only in the way."

"Why don't you just shut up, Dylan, and hear what she has to say? Then you can run away if you must, but not until."

He'd never heard Cam so frustrated before. "Okay. I'll listen." Looking down at her was killing him. He wanted her with all his heart. "Erica, what do you want to tell me?"

"Please, can we sit on the bed?" she asked sweetly.

He could feel her shaking against his body. "Of course."

"Please listen and don't stop me. I want to tell you everything."

He could feel her agony in the very fiber of his being. Pain was something he understood. "Erica, I'll do whatever you ask."

"It happened after my parents died..."

* * * *

Erica leaned into Dylan, exhausted from telling him the dark truth of her rape. Cam sat on the other side of her on the bed. This was where she belonged. *With them.* Even if she was damaged or not, they were her life now. She wasn't going to give up on them. She wasn't giving up on herself either.

Dylan brushed the hair out of her face. She looked into her own reflection on the lenses of his shades. How did he see her after hearing about her past?

"Say something, Dylan," she said.

"I'm so sorry you went through all of this. If I had known, I would've killed the motherfucker."

"No one knew. Just me and Mr. Boyd." She closed her eyes. "I don't think I'll really ever get over it. The asshole died before I could confront him. It feels unfinished to me."

"God, you are so strong, Erica Coleman." Dylan took off his sunglasses and tossed them to the side. "Much stronger than me. That's why I'm not good enough for you, baby."

"That's bullshit, and you know it."

"No. It isn't. I've done things that you can't even imagine."

"What things?" she asked, sensing ancient pain begin to bubble up inside him.

She knew it would be hard for him, as it had been for her, but forcing the demons out and into the light was the only way to begin to heal. She'd learned that tonight. Dylan needed to learn that, too. Then they could have a chance at happiness.

Dylan took in a deep breath, continuing to stroke her hair. "I can tell you some things. No names, dates, or locations. That's classified."

"I don't need to know any of that. What I need to know is what caused you to think you're not good enough for me."

"I want to know, too." Cam's tone was of a concerned and loving brother.

"I was an assassin for the CIA." His eyes narrowed, but his gaze never left her. He was clearly waiting for a reaction from her.

Yes, she was a little shocked but not completely. "Dylan, I know whatever you did was for our country."

"That's what I always told myself." He sighed. "Most missions made sense to me. They were cut and dry. The targets were terrorists. Four years ago I was on a mission to take out a powerful financer of Al-Qaeda operatives. Everything was going as planned. He was in a hotel. The intel had stated he was alone. But he wasn't." Dylan's voice was steady, but it was obvious to her his words were slicing into his soul. His dark past had left him damaged, like her. "I came in through an open window. He was in bed asleep. As I shot him, his wife came out from the bathroom. She screamed. I turned, ready to exit back through where I'd come, but the woman was grabbing for a gun that was on the dresser. My training kicked in. I shot her."

"That was self-defense, Dylan. It couldn't be helped. You did what you had to do."

"That's what everyone at the Agency kept telling me during the debriefing. But it wasn't just the man's wife that witnessed my crime. Their four-year-old daughter, whom the woman had been bathing, ran into the room with a towel around her waist. She screamed as her mother dropped to the floor." Dylan closed his eyes. "I had to leave her, that innocent child. I ruined her life." He took in a deep breath and opened his eyes. "So you see, honey. I'm no good for anyone, especially you."

Erica's heart broke in two for Dylan. She didn't have any words to help him. All she could do was hold him and pray his demons would go away.

Chapter Thirteen

Cam put his arm around Erica, who was holding on to his brother with both hands.

"This won't work," Dylan said. "I'm not the man for you. Cam is."

"That's not true. You're a good man," she told him. "I'm the one who caused this. You guys deserve someone who isn't so messed up as I am."

"That's it." Cam stood up and looked down at the pair. "You two are really starting to piss me off."

"What's wrong?" Erica asked, her eyes wide in surprise.

"Let me spell it out for you. A. You're a survivor, though you doubt yourself too much. What you've been through would've driven most to the insane asylum, but not you. You are still standing. Losing your parents didn't knock you down for good. You got on your feet and started thinking about your brothers and the other orphans. What happened with that asshole, Boyd, didn't keep you down. You kept on putting one foot in front of the other. Even what happened at TBK Tower and your abduction shook you but didn't change who you are. You, Erica Coleman, are the most amazing, beautiful, strong woman I've ever known. Are you hearing me?"

"Yes," she whispered, the hint of a smile on her lips.

Cam turned to Dylan. "Now B. You're full of crap, big brother. You're a fucking hero, not a criminal. Yes, what happened to that kid was horrific, but that's just life. Shit happens. You were doing your duty. Who knows how many children's lives you saved that day by taking out that creep?"

"Is there a C. to this, Cam?" Dylan asked, the light coming back into his eyes.

"Damn right there's a C. The three of us need each other. You two understand what it means to carry a darkness around in secret for years."

Dylan turned to Erica. "He's right about that."

"Yes, he is."

"We're finally getting somewhere," Cam said.

"Finish your closing argument, bro."

"You bet I will. D. You need each other. E. You both need me. I'm the one who knew from the very beginning that we belonged together. F—"

"Wait." Erica stood and wrapped her arms around his neck. "And F. I love you, Cameron Strange."

"And I love you." He crushed his mouth to hers, feeling his future on her lips.

Dylan stood beside her. "G. I love you, Erica Coleman."

She turned to him. "I love you, Dylan."

His brother pulled her in tight and devoured her lips.

When they ended their kiss, Dylan looked at him. "And H. You're the best fucking brother a man could ever have." Then, out of the norm for Dylan, he gave him a bear hug.

* * * *

Erica felt the weight of the world lift off her shoulders. Cam and Dylan had freed her of the darkness inside. Hearing Dylan's tragic story had softened her heart. Listening to Cam's logic had finished the job. She was theirs and they were hers. Inside, her light began to burn bright again. But she knew that she could withdraw back into the shadows if she let herself. Dylan, too, might slip into that dark space of his. That was not going to happen. From now on, her job was to make both her men happy and in turn that would make her happy, too.

Dylan wrapped her up in his arms. He was open to her like never before. The sunglasses were off and his secrets were out. “I love you,” he whispered, kissing her neck.

This was where she belonged. With the Strange brothers.

They’d shown her that she was stronger than she thought. There were things she could control and things she couldn’t. Boyd wasn’t her fault. She was a child. Her parents’ death wasn’t something she could stop. It had been a tragic accident. The incident at TBK Tower a few months ago with the maniac who had gotten past her desk wasn’t her fault either. He had a gun. She hadn’t. She’d even done her best when the two Russians had abducted her. Knowing what she could control and what she couldn’t was the key. Now, she could heal and move on into the rest of her life.

She turned her head slightly to Cam, who was only a fingertip away, taking in his delicious manly sight. In his Levi’s and boots, he looked more cowboy than counselor. In the courtroom, Cam wore his lawyer garb, which was absolute seductive perfection—silk tie, Italian suit. But now, the way he was dressed and acting, Cam was the epitome of male beauty.

Dylan, the man in black and mirrored sunshades, would make any woman’s heart flutter. But here, now, raw and exposed, he was sexy as fucking hell.

She knew exactly what she wanted—*needed.* They needed it, too. “I want you two. Please. Make love to me again.”

“Your pleasure is our pleasure,” Cam said, feathering his fingers over her shoulders. “You’re so beautiful.”

“Sexy, too.” Dylan stood in front of her with his dark hair—normally never out of place—ruffled and messy.

“You two are free with the compliments. That’s for sure. I’m average, maybe even above average in some places, but not beautiful and definitely not sexy.”

Dylan pressed his mouth to hers, his tongue tracing her lips. Her toes curled and her insides tingled. Without him and Cam, she would've remained lost. Knowing how they saw her, made her feel strong and warm…and yes, even beautiful and sexy.

Cam was cupping her shoulders and kissing her neck. "You have no idea how hard it was working with you at TBK and imagining you between me and my brother like this."

Dylan released her lips. "Me, too, counselor. You're legal. You only see her from time to time. I had to see her almost every day, checking on security."

"Please don't go back to the CIA." She reached up and put her arms around his neck. "Matt and Sean said your old boss, a Mr. Black, was trying to get you to go back. Don't."

"Well, Miss Coleman. He made me a pretty good offer. What's your offer to get me to stay in Destiny?"

"This." She unbuttoned his shirt and parted it, exposing his muscled chest. "And this." She leaned into him and kissed his nipples. "And this." She knelt down in front of him, unbuckled his belt and unfastened his slacks. She'd never been so wanton and forceful, but she was enjoying herself, enjoying the hot glances he and Cam were giving her from above. "This." She unzipped Dylan's pants. He wasn't commando but he also didn't wear briefs or boxers. "A jock strap?"

"Does that surprise you, baby?" He smiled. "A man never knows when he has to chase someone or if he's about to be chased. A jock strap is the best protection for my balls. You were telling me about your offer?"

"Yes, I was." She looked up at the two brothers who were standing shoulder to shoulder. "The offer is for both of you, gentlemen."

"Gentlemen?" Cam laughed. "Hardly."

She reached over and cupped his cock through his jeans. "Wait until you hear everything before you make your decisions."

"You got a deal, baby." Cam touched her on the cheek. "But you've already sold me."

"Me, too," Dylan confessed.

She loved that they were enjoying this, enjoying her. They'd saved her from the Russians. They'd saved her from her demons. They deserved her best, and she was going to give it to them, give all of herself to them.

She pulled down Dylan's pants to his ankles. He lifted his legs and kicked them to the corner, and then he tossed his shirt to the floor. He was in his shoes and jockstrap, which wasn't able to keep even half of his hard ten-inch cock contained. He looked deliciously sexy. She put her index finger on the tip of his dick and found a pearly drop. She brought it up to her lips, tasting Dylan's essence.

Cam wasn't waiting for her to strip him. He was out of his clothes and boxers in a flash. She loved his lusty impatience. Loved him. His hand was on his cock. She leaned forward and licked him up and down his monstrous, long shaft.

While she was pleasuring Cam, Dylan kicked off his shoes and socks and removed his jockstrap. Now the two men stood in front of her like Greek Olympians. Powerful. Strong. Mighty. Hot.

Dylan's hands threaded through her hair. "I think you have the better offer than Mr. Black, sweetheart. Much better, but I'd like to see more. Strip for me. I want to see all your assets on display."

Cam nodded. "Now you're talking my language, bro."

She rose to her feet. Warmth spread through her. She removed her top slowly, hoping to get under their skin. Their hot eyes, which were locked in on her, told her she'd succeeded. Bare above the waist except for her bra, she moved to her slacks and unfastened the top button. Their heavy breathing was driving her wild. She'd never felt sexier in her life.

"Damn, you're hot." Cam's voice came from deep in his chest. "You're the hottest woman I've ever seen."

"I've never wanted anyone more than I want you right now." Dylan growled. "Get on with the show, sweetheart."

She was having fun. It felt good to make them squirm. They sure had made her squirm over the years. Turnabout was fair play. She removed her sandals. A shiver rolled up and down her spine as she removed her slacks. Dylan had taken her panties earlier, so she was bare underneath.

Standing in front of them in only her bra, she glanced at the mirror behind them on the dresser. Her reflection surprised her. She'd never looked better. Dylan and Cam had brought that out in her. They were all meant to be together, just like Cam had known for some time.

"That's it," Cam snapped and stepped forward.

"What's wrong?" she asked, trembling at his sudden outburst.

"Nothing, baby. I'm just done waiting." Cam cupped her breasts with his big hands. "Damn, your breasts are so perfect. You're perfect."

"To you, maybe."

"Yes, to me." She loved having Cam caress her this way. A hot sizzling line shot from where he touched her down to her pussy. She was getting wet. Very wet.

"Fuck, I'm done waiting. Your offer is too fucking good. I'm staying, Erica. I'm not going to the CIA. I'm staying with you and Cam in Destiny." Dylan came up behind her and reached around, his fingers finding her pussy. She moaned loudly when he touched her clit, the pressure inside her multiplying.

She leaned her head against Cam's chest and reached behind, needing to touch them both, to complete the circuit of electricity they were raising inside her.

"This is where you belong, Erica," Dylan said. "Between me and Cam."

* * * *

Dylan pressed his lips to Erica's neck and continued fingering her sweet pussy.

Gone was the suffering he'd felt that had started back at the beach when she'd screamed. It had vanished soon after she and Cam had knocked on the door. She was what he needed. Because of her, he'd shared his dark truth, something he'd never done before outside of the report he'd filed at the Agency. Because of her, he and Cam were closer than they'd ever been. They were sharing her. Erica. The woman they would spend the rest of their lives with.

Every day that he walked past her desk at TBK had added to his desire for her. He'd resisted, thinking it could never be. Then when she'd asked him to give her self-defense lessons and to teach her to shoot, his hunger for her had grown and grown. She saw herself as weak and frightened. She wasn't. She was strong and courageous. Hell, she had more guts than anyone he'd ever known, and that included himself.

He inhaled her essence. A sweet jasmine with a hint of honey. Her scent went all the way down into his dick.

"I want you both," she confessed, breathily. "Like we did at the beach."

"Your wish is our command, baby," Cam said, reaching down to retrieve his jeans. He pulled out two condoms and a little tube of lube. "But I want to feel your tight pussy around my dick this time." Cam handed the lubricant to him and one of the foil packages.

"And I want to claim your gorgeous ass for myself," he told her.

She moaned, which was the sweetest sound he'd ever heard. He saw her reflection in the mirror behind them out of the corner of his eye. He tilted his head that direction to get a better look. She was sandwiched between him and Cam, the image of feminine perfection. Every part of him wanted her, wanted to devour her. His cock throbbed and his balls ached like mad.

He nuzzled her neck with his face and moved his left hand to her ass. "This is mine."

She trembled against him, making him even harder and hungrier. He ripped open the condom package while Cam continued to caress her.

After Dylan had his cock fully sheathed, he broke the tiny seal on the tube and squeezed out the lubricant onto his hands. He applied the slick stuff to her ass, stretching her out to make her ready for his cock. God, he wanted this, wanted her. There was something so right about being with her and claiming her in this intimate way.

As Cam put on the rubber, Dylan reached around Erica and fondled her chest. Her breasts were soft and full, just the way he loved them. "You're mine, baby. All mine."

"And mine," Cam said, pulling her onto the bed on top of him. They kissed each other.

These two people were his life now and forever. He stared down at Erica's tempting ass and crawled on top of her. He and Cam were in sync like never before. Without a word, they both entered her body at the same time.

"Yes. God, yes." She was so wonderfully tight, and the shivers he felt from her were driving him wild.

Every thrust he sent into her was filled with possessiveness. *Mine. She's mine.* In and out. He and Cam were claiming her, making her theirs. In and out. Over and over. He could sense her approaching climax, which fueled his raging fire inside him. Harder. Faster. Deeper. In and out. She was his. This moment was all that mattered. With her. With Cam. In and out. His breaths sawed in and out of his chest, deepening. *I will never let her go.*

Cam groaned, clearly shooting his load.

"Cam. Dylan. Yes. Yes. Yes." Erica's orgasm pushed him over the edge.

"Fuuuck!" He shoved his cock all the way inside her ass, which was tightening around his shaft. It was as if his entire body had found release as he came inside the woman of his dreams.

* * * *

Erica loved being between Cam and Dylan. They'd fallen asleep shortly after their lovemaking. She'd remained wide awake, vibrating from the joy she felt inside her.

No matter where in the world she went, with these two wonderful men by her side, she was safe and at home.

Dylan kissed her hair. "How are you, baby?"

"I've never been better, handsome."

"I love you." Hearing those three words from him sent her to the moon. But the next words that fell from his mouth filled her with anxiety. "I can't wait to show you off at Phase Four."

Could she be the sub these two Doms deserved? After everything that they'd done for her, she had to try.

Chapter Fourteen

Cam looked around the small diner in Goodnight, Colorado. It was nice enough, but it didn't feel like home. He'd just finished his breakfast, which was only fair. The gravy was instant, unlike back home at Blue's. It was filling, so he couldn't complain.

Erica and Dylan were across from him in the booth, still working on their food. Erica's blue eyes were sparkling this morning. Dylan's couldn't be seen, since he was back in his shades, but the ease in his manner told Cam he was happy things had worked out the way they had.

Cam couldn't help but smile. This was going to be the rest of his life, being with Erica, sharing her with his brother. What more could he ask for? *Nothing.*

He did want that fucking Russian who'd been responsible for Erica's abduction behind bars where he belonged. He also wanted the ten million in ransom the Knights had sent to be returned. The issue with Kip Lunceford was still on the back burner. That needed to be resolved. Matt and Sean were weeding out the destructive code Lunceford had gotten into TBK's network. Other than that, life was perfect.

He reached across the table and grabbed Erica's hand. She smiled at him. *Really perfect.*

He heard a buzzing noise and reached for his cell. He came up empty. "Not me." He would have to remember to look for it once they were back in Destiny. He definitely didn't want to buy a new cell.

"It's me," Dylan said, and pulled out his phone. "This is Strange."

Erica sipped on her coffee. God, she was so gorgeous. What a night they'd had. This was just the beginning of their life together.

"We will have her there in an hour," Dylan told the person on the other end of the call, and then he clicked off his cell and tucked it back into his coat.

Erica turned to him with a questioning look on her face.

"We need to get the ticket and get back to Destiny." Dylan grinned.

"Who was that?" she asked. "Was it one of the Knight brothers?"

"Still the inquisitive one, aren't you, baby?" Dylan shook his head. "No. It wasn't. I did get a text from them this morning though. I'm on strict orders to keep you away from the office today. And you don't want me and Cam to lose our jobs, do you?"

Cam liked the lightness in his brother. It had been years since he'd seen Dylan act this way. Erica was the reason for the change in him.

"Of course not," she said. "But I have so much to do."

"TBK can survive without its powerhouse woman for one day," Dylan said.

"But—"

"No 'buts,' baby." Dylan put his arm around her shoulders and pulled her in tight. "Except your pretty ass.

"Cam, back me up, please."

"Sorry, sweetheart. I need my job. Besides, I think a little time off for all of us is a very good idea. I cut my leave by half of the time requested. I have some ideas on how the three of us can spend the rest of this vacation, and it starts with your gorgeous butt." He sent her a wicked wink.

"You two are in a conspiracy. I don't have a chance."

"No, you don't," Dylan said. "Besides, we have other orders from the biggest brass in Destiny."

She tilted her head to the side. "Biggest brass?"

"The women. We're supposed to deliver you to them, pronto."

Cam chuckled. "We better get going."

"When we get back to Destiny, I need to make a stop at my house before we drop her off," Dylan said conspiratorially. "I have something for Erica."

"What?" she asked.

"You'll have to wait and see."

* * * *

Dylan came out of his house with Erica's gift. Cam had driven his car back alone, insisting that she needed to spend more time with him. If Cam hadn't spent so much time getting his law degree, he would've made one hell of a psychologist and given Sam O'Leary a run for his money.

The ride back with Erica had been one of the best times in his life. Too bad the trip wasn't longer. Cam's car was parked behind his. Waiting on him, Cam and Erica were standing on the sidewalk in front of his house.

"I'm dying to know what this is about, Dylan Strange." God, she was the most beautiful woman he'd ever seen.

"Here you go," he said, holding the giftwrapped box for her.

"It's not my birthday. What's the occasion?"

He shrugged. "Cam told me about how you did at the Knights' gun range. Call this a celebration for doing so well. Three shots hit your target. That's really good."

"How many bullets were in that clip?" she asked. "Ten or more. That's pretty bad odds."

"Honey, you did great." He was proud of her. How many people could've gone through what she'd had to endure and been able to keep sane? "We're going to keep up your lessons."

"Open it up, baby," Cam said. "I'm dying of curiosity. Dylan has never been someone to give gifts. I count myself lucky to get a birthday card every other year."

"Hey, that's not true. I got you fishing gear last year."

"Right. That was for Christmas. Remember? And you only bought it because you wanted to go with me, which by the way, hasn't happened yet."

"It will. I swear." Dylan handed the present to her.

Without hesitation, she ripped into the package. Her eyes widened when she saw what was inside. "It's a gun."

"Yes, it is. The Glock was too much weapon for you."

"The handle is pinkish," she said, pulling it out carefully. "It looks too pretty to be a gun."

"It's not loaded. There are some bullets in the bottom of the box. You can practice with it the next time we are at the Knights gun range."

"Thank you, Dylan. I love it." She got up on her tiptoes.

He bent down and kissed her. "The ladies will skin me alive if I don't get you to the party."

"Party?"

Dylan smiled knowing that Erica was in for an afternoon of fun.

* * * *

Erica walked into Betty's Beauty Shop with Dylan and Cam and was ambushed by a bunch of women. "What's this all about?"

They all started laughing and rushed to her with hugs and smiles.

Ethel smiled. "We're celebrating Nicole's upcoming nuptials."

She looked at the faces, all of them her friends.

Amber, the Stone brothers' lady, stood next to her sister, Belle.

Megan, the Knights' woman, held a glass of champagne for her. "This is for you."

"It's not even ten in the morning," she said.

"It's past five in England, love," Gretchen said in her familiar British accent. "This is a party, Erica."

One week ago today, she was in the trunk of a car, unsure if she would live to see another day. Next week she had to face the memorial service and remembering that day so many years ago when her life changed forever. She needed a day to be happy.

"That sounds lovely," Erica said and took the glass.

"I think you ladies have things under control here," Dylan said. "One of us will be right outside if you need us."

"Shoo, young man," Betty, the owner of the shop, said. Middle-aged and plump, the redhead always wore her hair up.

"Yes, ma'am." He and Cam walked out the door, leaving her to these wonderful conspirators.

Erica had formed a bond years ago with Betty and her daughter, Kaylyn. "How's Snow?"

Snow was the first puppy Erica had ever saved. Betty had adopted him and given the sweet dog a great home.

"Snow is a tough old boy. He's still got that spark you saw when you found him. You should come see him, sweetie."

"I will." Erica thought a trip out to the ten acres that Betty had set up for Kaylyn's service dog school would be just what she needed to lift her spirits. "How is Kaylyn doing?"

"She's got five great dogs ready to go. Did your brothers tell you that she's got a beautiful German shepherd she's training for Nicole's friend who lost his sight at that shooting in the park? What was his name?"

"Jaris," Erica reminded Betty.

"That's it. Jaris is still training in Denver to adapt to his blindness. The guy who is working with him is a longtime friend of ours. Chance was born blind. We keep trying to get him to come work for us with the service dogs. Kaylyn won't give up asking. One thing about my daughter, she's persistent."

"Yes, she is."

"I've always thought those two had feelings for each other. Not sure what's holding them back."

"Betty, don't go meddling in Kaylyn's life," she said with a giggle. "Remember how bad it turned out when you set up Phoebe with Andy McCrae."

"I thought for sure they would be perfect for one another. I wouldn't dream of playing matchmaker with Kaylyn. But if you have any suggestion that might move things along for those two, come sit by me."

"You're a little devil, Betty Anderson."

Betty smiled. "Erica Coleman, you behave."

The woman was one of the sweetest women in Destiny. "What's Jaris's dog's name?"

"Sugar. She's a lovely dog. Jet black. She'll be fully trained by the time Jaris is ready to come get her."

"Nicole will be happy about that. The work you and Kaylyn are doing is so important."

"It's more Kaylyn than me, honey. I'm an old hair burner from way back. She does all the training for the service dog school. I just love on the puppies."

"An important job, too, Betty." She hugged the woman. "I promise to come see you soon."

Paris walked up. "I'm so glad you're safe, Erica."

"Thank you. How are you doing?" she asked. Being a nurse, the poor girl had been in the fire at the clinic and would've died if not for Erica's brothers' firefighting skills.

"It's been a while since the clinic burned down. I'm doing much better. You're the one who's been through hell."

Erica sighed. "I'm doing okay. Really I am."

"What happened to you won't just vanish, Erica." Kelly, the young hairdresser who worked for Betty, shook her head. "I know. It stays with you. Always."

Erica was about to ask her what had happened to her when the door opened and Phoebe rushed in, her arms loaded with snacks.

"Sorry, I'm late," Phoebe said. "I had to take Shane to Doc Ryder to get him checked out. He's fine, but I had to be sure." Even though she was the youngest of the Blue children, Phoebe was a bit of a mother hen when it came to both her brothers, but especially Shane.

"When I picked up Mom and the food, Mom was running late. She'll be here shortly. Is Nicole here yet?"

"You beat her," Erica said, warming up to the excitement. Maybe it was a good idea to take some time off from work. This was a great way to start. Nicole was going to be her brothers' wife in a month. Their fiancée was already like a sister to Erica.

"I'm sure Destiny's sweet deputy will love this day of beauty," Gretchen said.

"We all will," Belle, Amber's sister, added, looking in the mirror and running her fingers through her hair. "I could definitely benefit from a new hairstyle."

"Are you kidding?" Paris said, shaking her dark hair. "I would love to have your blonde hair. It looks beautiful."

"I love you hair, Paris." Erica loved the woman's soft dark pixie cut.

"I've been thinking about letting it grow out and lightening it a lot."

"You can," Betty said. "Kelly is a genius when it comes to color."

Nicole came through the door wearing her uniform, her gun by her side. Erica thought she looked so beautiful and powerful.

"Surprise!" they all said in unison.

Nicole smiled. "Jason sent me here to check on a possible break-in. A broken latch? I'm betting there isn't one. He was in on this, wasn't he?"

"Everyone in Destiny was in on it, love." Gretchen handed Nicole a glass of champagne. "Haven't you figured out how things work around here yet?"

"I'm still on duty," Nicole told them.

"No you're not." Ethel grinned. "The minute you walked into Betty's place, you were off the clock."

"Okay," she said, taking the glass from Gretchen. "Let's party. Cheers, everyone."

"Cheers," they all said together.

It felt good to Erica to be home.

* * * *

The snow-covered peaks sparkled like jewels from the late afternoon sun's beams. The sky was dotted with puffy clouds. The air was the perfect temperature. Colorado had never looked better to Dylan.

He sat with Cam on the bench in the park, facing Betty's Beauty Shop, where the woman responsible for his new outlook was enjoying a day of beauty with some of the other women in Destiny.

Day of beauty? Erica was ravishing with or without makeup. She was a natural beauty both inside and out.

"My sesame chicken isn't going to hold me for too much longer," Cam said. Around noon, he'd gone into Phong's and brought back lunch for both of them. "I'm thinking we get some burgers from Lucy's for dinner."

"How much longer will Erica be in there?"

"Beats me, but I'm betting it will be a couple of hours at least." Cam grinned.

"More like four or five."

"Erica needs this. A day thinking about something other than what happened with the Russians. And Monday is the anniversary and memorial service. That's going to be rough."

Dylan agreed. "My money is on Ethel and Gretchen making sure she enjoys herself."

His cell buzzed.

"That's got to be you," Cam said. "I'm still without my phone."

He brought out his cell. "It's Black."

"He's going to be pissed that you're going to turn him down."

"Too bad for him," he told his brother. Then he spoke into the phone. "Strange here."

"Hey, buddy. I've got some good news and some bad news."

"Don't worry about it. I didn't think you could get me reinstated anyway. Besides, things have changed here for me. I'm staying."

"Fuck. That wasn't what I needed to hear. I didn't get the green light to bring you back, Dylan. Not yet. But everyone here knows your work. All I need is another week to remind them what you've done for this agency and they will be more than ready to get you back in the field."

The face of the child appeared in the back of Dylan's mind. "I'm never coming back, Black."

"I hate hearing that, but I understand."

"What's the good news?"

Black's voice came through loud and clear. "An agent in Russia found evidence that links Niklaus Mitrofanov to the Russian front company, Spetssetstorsky Construction."

"Got it." That was the business the Knights had bought into with the ten million ransom monies.

"My man has his hands on a laptop that has incriminating e-mails. They're from Mitrofanov to the president, who happens to be his cousin back in Russia, with details of the con. The agent is remote at the moment. Once he can upload an encrypted file to me, we'll have enough evidence to take down Mitrofanov."

"That's all I need, Black."

"Strange, don't make a move until I have the evidence in my hands."

That's not happening. Erica's safety was the most important thing to him. The sooner Mitrofanov was off the streets the better. "I'll handle things here. You let me know when you hear from your man." He clicked off his cell. "You stay here and keep a lookout on the shop."

"Where are you going?"

"Black just gave me enough to have Mitrofanov arrested. I'm going to get Jason and then we'll put that motherfucker in a cell."

* * * *

Erica's hair was damp from the shampooing that Kelly had just given her. "I only need a half inch off to get rid of my split ends."

"Got it. While I'm cutting, I want you to put your feet in here." Kelly pointed to the tub on the floor. "Nicole looks pretty, doesn't she?"

The way Kelly had done Nicole's updo looked stunning.

"She does," she said, placing her toes into the warm water. "Is that how she's going to wear her hair at the wedding?"

"She's still deciding. Erica, I hope you don't mind being my last customer."

"Don't mind at all. I've had a great time."

By the table of food and drink near the back, Gretchen, who was on her third glass of champagne, was teaching the rest of the girls an old traditional English folk song about a man in love with a woman named Sally.

Ethel's cell rang and she stepped away from the chorus. She walked over to her and Kelly. "I've got to go and do something for Jason. I'll be right back after I finish. Keep an eye on Gretchen. Another glass of champagne and she'll be dancing on the table."

Ethel left and Kelly began clipping her hair. "You look so lovely and relaxed. After all you've been through, it's nice to see you this way."

"I've fallen in love with Cam and Dylan. Which has been wonderful for me. But I still have those moments—those horrible moments."

Kelly nodded. "That's going to go on for a while, I'm afraid to tell you." She lowered her voice to almost a whisper. "I've never told anyone in Destiny about what brought me here. It's something I've never wanted to talk about until now. I was kidnapped, too."

"I had no idea." Erica was glad to have someone who could really understand what she'd gone through. "You always give the impression of being so put together and upbeat."

"At first it was a façade, but now I really am better. I just wanted to let you know that as time passes the memory lessens."

"What about the nightmares?" Erica asked, thinking about her severe anxiety. She'd screamed because it had bubbled up from her subconscious, ruining what had been a perfect evening with Dylan and Cam at Lover's Beach.

"There's fewer of them, but I'm not sure they ever go away for good. I pray they will someday for you and me."

Like her, Kelly had been changed after her abduction. As they talked more, Erica recalled what Dylan had said at the motel room about taking her to Phase Four. Could she go there after everything that had happened? The guys had spanked her the night before on Lover's Beach. That hadn't been a problem for her. But the shirt coming over her head had sent her into a total panic. Could she submit totally, allow them to tie her down or blindfold her? Would that bring back the nightmares? She knew her guys were Doms through and through. Eventually she would need to try BDSM again. But she needed at least a few more days to get her head on straight.

But what if I'm not like Kelly? What if I stay screwed up like this for the rest of my life? What if I can't return to BDSM, the lifestyle of Cam and Dylan?

Kelly spun her around to face the mirror. "Will this work for you? I think your guys are going to love it."

Erica looked at her long dark hair. Kelly had shaped it perfectly, allowing it to fall just the way she liked it. "Thank you for the hair and for the talk. I needed both."

"I needed it as well, Erica. It's good to talk to someone who has been through what I've been through." Kelly leaned close and lowered her voice. "The one thing that has gotten me through some of my darkest points is to appreciate every single day. You can always find happiness if you know where to look."

"Sounds like you might be in love."

Kelly shook her head. “No, but you definitely are.”

Yes, I am. Whenever she looked into Cam’s and Dylan’s faces, she found her happiness. Somehow she was going to get past her hesitation about BDSM and be the woman they deserved.

Chapter Fifteen

Dylan stepped onto the porch of the house on Second Street that Mitrofanov had purchased two days ago.

Jason was beside him. He knocked on the door hard. “Open up. This is Sheriff Wolfe.”

It was time to get the rat out of his hometown and behind bars where he belonged. Ethel had signed the warrant and he and Jason had headed straight to this house to get the bastard.

Another hard knock by Jason shook the entire porch. “Get your ass out here, Niklaus. Now!” The sheriff's other hand was on his weapon.

Holding his own weapon, Dylan heard footsteps inside headed to the door. *Give me a reason, motherfucker. Any reason.* His heart was beating at the rate it always did before a kill. Steady. Very steady.

The door opened. It wasn't Niklaus. Too young.

“Where's your uncle?” Jason asked, apparently having met the guy. He had tats on his neck, a symbol of his mafia ties.

“He's not taking visitors now, Sheriff.”

“This isn't a social call.” Dylan pushed the man out of the way. As he walked past him, he reached into the punks jacket and freed him of his pistol. “Be smart. If you want to keep breathing, don't pull the knife that's strapped to your ankle.”

The guy's eyes widened in surprise, and he stepped back.

He and Jason had their guns out. *One reason. That's all.*

From a hallway, a short balding man, obviously Mitofanov, walked into the front room where they were standing. Behind him came another man, who looked to be the twin of the other.

"Sheriff Wolfe, what a pleasure to see you again so soon," the fucker said with a twisted smile.

"Hands up," Jason ordered. "Everyone."

Two more men appeared from where Niklaus and his henchman had come. They both wore suits, and Dylan recognized something in their eyes. They were killers—like him.

The odds weren't the best—five to two—but he'd seen worse and walked out alive.

One wrong move by any of them and he would take them out. Jason's gun was pointed at Niklaus. That took care of one target. The other four were his. The two assassins had to go down first. Then the neck-tatted thug that still had a gun would be next. The guy by the door with only a knife would be last. That would take less than two seconds, maybe three. Then he would empty the remaining two bullets into Niklaus, just in case Jason's shot wasn't a kill shot. The assessment of the situation and what had to be done took him less time than it took to take in a breath. It was like riding a bike.

Niklaus put his hands in the air. The other men did the same.

Damn.

Jason moved cautiously behind Mitrofanov. "I have a warrant for your arrest, Niklaus."

"Gentlemen, I think you may be…how you Americans say…getting the cart before the donkey."

Dylan kept his eyes tight on the other men in the room.

Jason put the cuffs on the mobster and read him his rights. "You're going away for a very long time."

"I doubt that, Sheriff. Before you take me to your jail, let me introduce you to my family. You've met my nephews, Gleb and Gerasim. These are my two living sons, Anton and Roman, Sergei's brothers. You remember Sergei, Sheriff. Don't you?"

"Shut up, asshole," Dylan barked.

"And who are you, sir?"

"The name's Strange."

"I see you took Gleb's gun." Niklaus pointed to the gun in his left hand.

"I did."

"I bet he wasn't even aware you snagged it from him, was he? I know a thing or two about picking pockets, but those criminal days are behind me, Strange. Why are you here? You're not an officer of the law are you?"

"I'm the guy who is going to see to it that you get locked up for good for what you did to Erica."

"Erica? Erica?" Niklaus's eyes narrowed. "Yes, I remember her. Is she your *podruga*?"

Dylan didn't answer the scumbag, though he spoke Russian and several other languages fluently and knew the word meant "girlfriend." He wasn't about to give Mitrofanov any information about Erica. *She's much more than my girlfriend, asshole. She's my life.*

* * * *

Erica and Nicole were enjoying a quiet Saturday afternoon alone at the cabin. Erica's brothers, Sawyer and Reed, built it years ago after their parents died. Now, they were building a real home for them and Nicole.

With Mitrofanov's arrest the day before, Dylan and Cam had lessened their bodyguard duties for her. They'd headed back to town ten minutes ago to buy some steaks that Cam promised to grill for tonight's dinner. It was nice to have alone time with Nicole.

Sawyer and Reed were shoeing their horses in the barn, which was a hundred yards to the left of a single-building construction site.

"The new house is coming along nicely, Nicole."

"I think so, too. Another three months and we should be able to move in. Of course, we'll have to save up to buy furniture."

"I'm sure my brothers would be satisfied with recliners and a giant flat screen."

"You're right about that." Her soon-to-be sister-in-law was out of uniform and looked so at ease. "Did I tell you that we spotted Connie again?"

Connie was the mountain lion that held a special place in all their hearts. "No. When?"

"Last week on Friday morning, but there was no sign of Charlie, her mate."

"Friday morning, huh." Erica's gut clenched. "The day I got taken."

"I'm sorry I reminded you of that," Nicole said. "I can't imagine what you're going through."

"You've also had your demons to contend with. And look at you? Strong. Powerful. Come what may, you take care of it." Erica sighed. "I wish I was more like you."

"We're more alike than you think." Nicole leaned forward in her chair. "You're every bit as strong and powerful as I am. Don't let those two guys of yours fool you into believing you're helpless. You're not."

"Cam and Dylan wouldn't do that. Believe me, they actually think I'm some kind of female superhero."

"They're right, too. By the way, how did you get them to relax the guard duty? I was surprised to see them drive away and leave you all alone, even with an officer of the law like me. Cam? Maybe. But Dylan? I would've never guessed he'd let you out of his sight."

"What about my brothers? They're overprotective with you, too. I remember how they were when you came to town. Have you forgotten?"

Nicole laughed. "No. Even now, they insist on checking up on me when I'm on duty. I've told them not to, but they just keep on doing it. I can shoot the wings off a fly at forty paces, but does that make them back down? No."

"You told me something about a moth not a fly, didn't you?"

Erica teased. "Isn't that what got you three going in the right direction in the first place?"

"Don't you tell another soul, Erica Coleman. I told you that in confidence." Nicole shook her head. "You Colemans are a lot alike."

"Don't hold it against me, please."

"I won't. How are the self-defense lessons going?"

She shrugged. "Okay. We went to the range again this morning before coming out here. And then after that, we went up the mountain a little and I practiced shooting moving targets. I'm not sure I'll ever be good with a gun, but Dylan gave me a new one. It's really cute. It's much smaller and has a pretty pink handle. I don't shake near as bad when I aim it, but it still feels a little odd in my hand."

Dylan had taught her some self-defense techniques. She'd spent the morning practicing her stance. Her men had seemed very proud of her. They said she was getting very adept.

When Dylan had deemed her ready, they'd moved on to what he called "phase two."

She'd practiced on Cam, using a paintball gun to track him through the trees. She was proud of the amount of blue paint that covered Cam when they'd finished.

"Give it time. The more you practice, the easier it will be."

Time?

That's what Kelly had told her at the beauty shop. The more time that passed, the easier it would get to face the kidnapping. But what Erica really wanted was more time with the Strange brothers. Much more time. Last night, she'd fallen asleep at Dylan's place, in his and Cam's arms. No sex. Just snuggling. Wonderful. They'd all been exhausted. The rest was welcomed.

Dylan hadn't mentioned going to Phase Four again, which took away some of her anxiety. More time. That was what she needed most.

As she and Nicole sipped on their lemonade, Erica could feel her muscles soften. Lazy days like this one felt good. Even before all this happened, she'd planned to take Monday off. Although she wouldn't attend the memorial service, she wanted to have the day to pay tribute to her parents. But she would be back to work Tuesday, whether Cam and Dylan approved or not. All three of them played key roles at TBK, and she wasn't about to leave Scott and Eric Knight hanging any longer. Matt and Sean were working hard to get Kip's nasty code out of the system. They could use Dylan's help with that. Cam, being head of legal, certainly had a ton to do. She wasn't sure how the Knights were doing without her, but she expected to find a pile of paperwork to get through. Besides, getting back to some of her old routines would help her heal. Of that, she was certain.

"I do want to ask a favor of you," Nicole said. "Will you be my maid of honor?"

"Oh Nicole, I would love to." Erica hugged the deputy of Swanson County, a woman who had become the sister she'd never had before.

Chapter Sixteen

Erica's insides were warm from the two glasses of wine Dylan had poured for her over dinner. Cam had cooked. She'd had no idea what a talented chef he was. He'd made several easy things for her last week when he'd stayed with her, but nothing like this.

The steaks he'd grilled at the cabin the night before had been amazing. Sawyer, Reed, and Nicole had kept going on and on about how good the food was and made Cam promise to do the same for their wedding reception. He'd agreed with a big smile on his face.

Tonight's lasagna was the best she'd ever had.

Right now, Cam and Dylan were in the kitchen cleaning up. She'd offered, but they'd insisted. God, what could be sexier than a man washing dishes? Two men washing dishes.

She grinned, happy that Cam and Dylan were taking such good care of her. After they'd left the cabin and gone to Cam's place last night, they'd crawled into bed and Dylan and Cam had taken turns making love to her. They'd all fallen asleep after in no time.

Today had been a whirlwind of activity. Breakfast at Blue's. Lunch at the O'Learys with all the other orphans. It had been a somber meal, all of them knowing what tomorrow would bring, until Patrick began recounting the dragon he swore he saw in China years ago. She'd heard the story a thousand times but never tired of it. The man was one of the sweetest she knew. Afterward, Cam and Dylan had taken her to a secluded area to test her on self-defense again. She'd gotten the jump on Cam this time, hitting him in the center of the chest with a splash of blue from the paintball gun Dylan had given her. She was exhausted. It would be good to be back to work on

Tuesday. She might get to slow down a little. Her guys sure kept her on her toes.

"You okay, baby?" Cam asked, poking his head through the pass-through into the kitchen.

"I'm great. You sure you don't need my help?"

He winked. "We've got it under control."

Control? That was a Dom's desire. Always. Cam and Dylan were Doms. She trembled, recalling Dylan's words about showing her off at Phase Four. Deep down, she wanted that more than anything. Wanted to give all of herself to them. But she still wasn't sure she could handle the things they would want to do to her. Doubt had stayed with her.

She'd always enjoyed being submissive in the bedroom and at the club before. Would she again?

Her mind kept replaying the incident at the beach. She didn't want to freak out again. Kelly had told her she needed time. She knew that was true. Time had softened the hurt of the loss of her parents. It had also made what happened with Boyd diminish, though that memory never had fully gone away. But she knew that time could only help so much. The shooting at TBK Tower and her abduction had caused her ancient scars to sting again, as if they'd been inflicted on her only yesterday.

"All done." Dylan walked back into the room.

"That was fast." She was still getting used to seeing him without his sunglasses. It made him look sexier to her, if that was even possible. He only took them off when it was just the three of them, and that made her feel very special.

He sat down beside her on the sofa. "I can be nice and slow, too, baby." He leaned in and kissed her, making her tingly all over. He deepened the kiss, sending his tongue into her mouth, and she felt her toes curl and a warm ball of desire in the center of her body.

Cam came out of the kitchen. "I see we're moving on to the next course."

She looked at the bottle of lubricant he was holding in his hand and felt her heart skip a beat.

"Yes, we are," Dylan told him.

I should be honest with them about my fears. Now's the time.

"Guys, I need to tell you—"

"The only thing that needs to happen now, sweetheart, is for Cam and me to get you out of your clothes." Dylan's dangerously hungry voice gave her a strange feeling in the pit of her stomach. She recognized it as a mix of anxiety and something else, something warm and delicious.

The cold remoteness he'd shown to her and the rest of the world was gone now. In Dylan's dark Dom eyes she could see how much he desired her, and that made her tremble. She slid her gaze to Cam, who looked just as fierce and sexy. Were they going to try a little D/s with her now? Wouldn't this—her house—be better suited to testing herself to see how far she could go rather than trying it at Phase Four? If she lost it here, it would be private. The only witnesses would be Cam and Dylan, once again. Freaking out at the club would leave her shamed and heading for the door. But what if she didn't go insane? What if her natural submissive side blossomed tonight? All the better. She would ask them to take her to Phase Four and have no worries. If the opposite occurred and she lost her mind tonight, she would tell them her truth. All of it. Her fears. Everything. She thought they would understand, but would they stay if she couldn't return to the lifestyle they practiced?

Dylan touched her cheek. His eyes were hot and unblinking. "Your mind drifted off, Erica. Where were you?"

She wasn't ready to tell him. Not yet. *Bring on the test, Sir.* "How much I like seeing you without your sunglasses."

"That will only happen here, baby."

"I know. I'm glad about that."

He smiled and covered her mouth with his. His arms came around her body, and he lifted her up off the sofa. She wrapped her legs around his waist and her arms around his neck, feeling her overwhelming need expanding inside her. He forced his tongue past her lips, dominating her with only a kiss. His mouth was ruthless, devouring every breath. She clung to him as if he was life itself. Her heart was racing and her body was shivering.

"It's definitely time for the next course," Cam said, his tone deepening to a sexy, lusty level.

"Where's he going?" she asked.

"Let's take this morsel to the bedroom."

Dylan took her hand. "Lead the way."

Her lips were throbbing like mad. She pressed her head into his chest as he followed Cam to the room they would claim her in again. She could hear his heartbeats pounding in his chest. Her hesitation was gone. Whatever they wanted from her, she would give it. She couldn't have stopped herself now, no matter the risk. Pressure was building inside her. Her skin was sizzling, plastered against him. Like a fortress's walls, he surrounded all of her.

Sensations flared inside her as heavy want to have him and Cam take her, fill her, and claim her flattened all her doubt. She groaned as her desperation expanded. She could feel her panties getting soaked by her dampening pussy. She kissed his chin, relishing the tickle of his five-o'clock stubble on her lips.

As Dylan lowered her to her bed, she felt her nipples beading terribly, her need to be touched, caressed, and filled multiplying with every heartbeat. Looking up at the two men on either side of her bed was making her wet and causing her clit to throb.

In a flash, they stripped her of all her clothes except her bra and panties.

"I thought you were going to go slow with me tonight." She leaned up and grabbed them both by the shirt and tugged. "Fair is fair." A button flew off of Cam's shirt. "Oops."

"You little devil. It's a good thing I know as much about a needle and thread as I do a knife and a spatula." He leaned down and crushed his lips to hers, and her pussy began to clench, her need to be filled so urgent. "Time to show you what I am capable of, baby."

She turned to look at Dylan. While Cam had been kissing her, he'd shucked all his clothes.

His urgency was clearly even greater than hers. "Let's get this show on the road." He bent down and kissed her pussy. She could feel his hunger, his possessiveness, his power against her most intimate flesh.

As Cam moved his lips to her neck, his left hand caressed her breasts and his other hand finished removing the rest of his clothing.

"Oh my God!" Her body was burning like crazy.

Dylan circled her clit with his tongue, increasing the amount of pressure inside her body. His hands were threading through her swollen folds, making her even wetter. Cam's mouth covered one of her nipples and he began sucking her into dizziness.

She was no longer breathing calmly, but every gasp was followed by a shaky moan.

Cam shifted up the bed. "I want to make love to your sweet lips, baby. Suck me. Make me feel you." He positioned his cock in front of her. She reached out with her fingertips and touched the bulbous head, finding a pearly drop on the slit. She brought it to her lips, tasting the precursor of his essence. "Delicious," she murmured, grabbing his shaft with her right hand and his balls with her left.

"Fuck, yes. That's it, darlin'." Cam's hands shot to the back of her head and he began stroking her hair.

Dylan's oral torture was about to send her over the top. She swallowed Cam's cock, taking in as much as she could. When it hit the back of her throat, she used her tongue on his dick and sucked hard on him until her cheeks hollowed out.

"Daaamn." Cam breathed out and tugged on her hair. "What a talented woman you are, baby."

When Dylan captured her clit with his tight lips and entered her pussy with one of his thick fingers, the pressure burst free, sending a flood of sensations through her body. The spasms in her pussy were mind blowing, and she could feel the release of more of her cream flow out of her body.

She could hear Dylan lapping up every drop. She sucked hard on Cam's cock as she felt it pulse in her mouth. Then she tasted his salty liquid hit the back of her throat.

Her whole body was on fire as the orgasmic quakes continued to shake all of her. Dylan moved up her body, dotting her skin with kisses along the way. Cam crawled up beside her, kissing her on the cheek. She was between them again, right where she belonged.

After a few breathless seconds, she turned to Dylan. "But you didn't come?"

He moved his hand back to her sex and sent a finger inside her. Her pussy clenched around it, but her desire for more was even greater. She needed them inside her in the worst way.

"That's my baby," Dylan said with a wicked grin. "I'm going to come tonight. I promise. Probably a few times. But so are you. Again and again and again."

Cam nodded. "My cock is already hard again. I'm ready to go, and I can tell that Erica is there, too."

Yes, I am. Right now, I feel like I could go all night.

Dylan rolled her on her side facing him. He devoured her lips again, and she felt a tingling line of desire zip through her. *I can never get enough of these men.*

Cam began applying lube to her ass, stretching her out, readying her backside for his cock.

She positioned her leg as high as possible on Dylan's hip, wanting to feel all of him inside her.

"I like you this way, baby," he said lustily. "Open for me. All of you. You're mine. You're mine."

"And mine," Cam said, kissing her neck from behind. She could feel both their cocks pressing against her body.

"Please," she begged. "I need to feel you inside."

They pierced her flesh, Dylan in her pussy and Cam in her ass, together, symphonically. The pressure rose inside her, expanding her cravings, her need, her desires. They were sending her to heaven with every lusty thrust. It was almost like an out-of-body experience that she never wanted to end. Her pulse burned in her veins and her heart raced in her chest. Her breathing was so shallow and uneven, unable to give her enough oxygen to keep her head from being dizzy. But she wanted more. So much more. Faster and faster, they sent their cocks into her pussy and ass. Over and over. She went higher and got hotter. More pressure. And still they drove into her, every plunge adding to her delicious suffering until she peaked, going over the edge of pleasure.

Dylan and Cam came inside her, their bodies stiffening as she tightened her insides around their cocks.

A million sensations fired inside her body. "Yes. God. Yes." The collision of Dylan and Cam inside her had brought her to this place—a place of release so thrilling, so complete, and so wonderful. All her energy was gone and she could sense the same was true in them. Her body began to shiver rapidly as they wrapped their arms around her, holding her tight in their embrace.

* * * *

Erica yawned, having dozed off for a little bit. Dylan was up on his elbows, staring down at her. She looked over her shoulder, expecting to find the other man she loved. "Where's Cam?"

"He went to get us some food. Thought you would be starving."

Even after the big dinner he'd made for them, she was a little hungry.

Dylan squeezed her hand. "I can't believe I found you, Erica."

"We found each other," she told him, reaching up and tracing his square jaw with her fingertips.

Cam walked in with a tray of food that would've fed a small

army. "We've got cheese and crackers, grapes and bananas. I brought us three bottled waters, but if you'd like me to open another bottle of wine, I can go back and get it."

"This is wonderful, Cam." She sat up, and Dylan fluffed a pillow for her back. "You know I've never eaten in this bed before. Actually, I've never eaten in any bed before. You two sure are spoiling me."

"More to come, sweetheart," Cam said, setting the tray down on the mattress and crawling in next to her.

Dylan handed her a cracker with a sliver of sharp cheddar. Cam opened her bottle for her. They all ate the food Cam had brought in silence. She looked at her two naked men and then glanced down at her bare chest. It felt completely wonderful being here with them this way. She'd always been shy about her body, having grown up in the O'Learys' house with her brothers. Now, with Cam and Dylan, it seemed so right to be naked with them.

"You're so beautiful, baby," Dylan said. "I can't wait to show you off at Phase Four."

She instantly tensed. *Why didn't I tell them before? Why did I wait?*

Cam stared at her. "What's wrong, Erica?"

God, he could see into her like no one before. "It's difficult for me to say. This is hard."

"What's hard?" Dylan cupped her chin. "It's just us, baby. You can trust us. Take your time. We're here for you."

"I'm sorry about what happened at the beach."

Dylan's eyes narrowed. "That wasn't your fault."

"I know, but I wish I hadn't hurt you."

"I'm not hurt now." Dylan kissed her forehead. "I've loved you for years, Erica. You have always been life to me, and being the fool I am, I steered clear."

"Why?" she asked.

"Because I never really expected this to happen. I've seen a ton of action in my day, but nothing scared the shit out of me more than you.

Now, I can't imagine not being with you, holding you like this. When you screamed after I pulled down your top over your head, I thought I'd lost you for good."

"I want this. I do. I know I'm waffling, but I can't help it. You both are into BDSM." She took a deep breath and then blurted out the truth of her hesitation. "I'm not sure I can be again after all that has happened to me. I don't know if I can handle being tied down or blindfolded."

Dylan smiled. "That's okay, baby."

"No. It isn't. That's your world. It isn't fair of me to ask you to give it up. I won't. It's not right."

"I think your mind is what's getting you into trouble, sweetheart," Cam said. "BDSM is something we've enjoyed. We know the ins and outs like the backs of our hands. That's true, too. But you, Erica, are the most important person in our lives now. We can put our lifestyle on the shelf. Later, when you're ready, we can take it one step at a time."

Dylan nodded. "If it doesn't work, then we enjoy the best vanilla sex the world has ever known."

They would do that for her and more. They'd already proven what lengths they would go to for her. But it wasn't right. Though the selfish side of her wanted to surrender to their selfless offer, how could she?

"Wouldn't that be a kind of half life? In the end, you would resent me. My heart would break in two." She closed her eyes. "I love you both. I love you so much I know I can never ask that of you. You're Doms. Don't deny it."

"Look at me, Erica," Dylan told her.

She opened her eyes and found his warm gaze locked in on her. "Yes?"

He took in a big breath. What was he going to say? Was this good-bye? It should be, but selfish or not, she didn't want it to be.

"We're both fucked up, aren't we?" He grinned. "Cam is right, baby. The only way to heal our darkness is to be together. You think you're pushing me and Cam away right now for us, but deep down it's your old demons creeping back up, screaming at you how worthless you are, aren't they?"

Like Cam, he seemed to be able to read her mind. "Yes."

Dylan grabbed her hands and brought them up to his chest. "My heart will always be yours, Erica." His dark eyes were solemn. "I love you. BDSM is something I enjoy, but you are the one I love. Do you understand?"

Her heart swelled. "Yes, but—"

"No 'buts.'" He put his finger to her lips. "Okay?"

She nodded and leaned her head into his shoulder. Cam kissed the back of her neck. She trusted them with everything, even her heart.

Chapter Seventeen

Cam hated seeing the pain on Erica's face. Dylan had left ten minutes ago to attend the annual memorial.

He looked at the time on his cell. The service would be starting in five minutes.

"Would you like something to drink, sweetheart?" he asked.

She shook her head.

He still wasn't sure why Dylan had agreed to go. His brother definitely was up to his old ways, working on a plan no doubt. What? He wasn't sure.

God, how he wished there was something to say to her to take away her pain. But there were no words. All he could do was be there for her.

He put his arm around her shoulder. She leaned her head into his chest.

Next year, I'll make sure we aren't in Destiny. He knew it wouldn't take away all her suffering, but he hoped it would lessen it.

* * * *

The sun had dipped behind the peaks and the sky's hue above the cemetery was deepening to purple.

Almost every citizen of Destiny was gathered around the graveyard, as they were every year at this same time. The tragedy of September 28, 2001 had changed the whole town, but especially the ones who had lost their parents. Dylan's mind was on the only missing orphan. *Erica.*

Holding an unlit candle, he stood by her parents' graves with her brothers, Reed and Sawyer, and their fiancée Nicole.

To the right of the large ceremonial candle, which was the only lit one in the entire cemetery, stood Patrick O'Leary. He had a microphone in his hand. His brother Sam and their wife Ethel were right behind him.

"We will never forget the plane crashing on that terrible September day," Patrick said solemnly. "The innocent ones we lost left an emptiness…"

As the speech continued, Dylan looked at the rest of the orphans. The Stones stood by their parents' graves. Emmett had his arm around Amber. Cody and Bryant had their hats in their hands. Megan was between Scott and Eric, who were next to the headstone of their parents.

Erica hasn't been here since that first service in 2001. The void that he felt in his heart for her absence was clearly felt by others, too. He could live with that, but he couldn't live with the agony she continued to carry.

"…each person was a friend, a family member, a light. As has been our practice since that horrific day on this anniversary, let us light our candles and take a moment of silence to remember our fallen."

As was always the practice, the orphans were the only ones to light their candles from the center one. They lit all the other candles.

After Reed lit his candle, Dylan moved through the many headstones, looking for the one he'd asked the location of from the caretaker earlier. A couple of rows from the rest of the crowd, he came to another grave. As the lighting of the candles and silence continued, his plan to help the orphan who he was madly in love with came into focus.

* * * *

Erica sat in Cam's car. She'd missed the memorial service again this year, unable to face the monster buried near her parents.

Although time had lessened the painful memories of that day twelve years before, it was still always hard for her. Today had been somewhat easier than the ones before because Cam had stayed by her side.

"Where are we meeting Dylan?"

"You'll see." Cam's demeanor had changed since getting the call from Dylan. Something was up, but she wasn't sure what.

They crossed over Silver Spoon Bridge, leaving the city limits of Destiny. Trying to tamp down her curiosity, she looked out at the moonlit peaks that had surrounded her all of her life. Destiny was home to her now more than it had ever been. Cam and Dylan were much like these mountains—tall, majestic, and beautiful.

Cam turned on Whispering Oaks Lane.

That road led to only one destination. She tensed, finding it odd that Cam was driving her there. "We're meeting him at the cemetery?"

Cam nodded. "Destiny Cemetery is our final destination."

"I know that, but I'm in no rush to go there. The memorial service should have already ended anyway. It's too late for me to attend." Were he and Dylan trying to force her to see her parents' graves and have some kind of epiphany? Her heart was racing.

"It's our final destination for today. You remember Dylan telling you he had a plan to help you with your demons?"

"I don't need to face anything. You've already helped me. You and Dylan." It was difficult to be here again.

"More to come, baby. More to come."

"No. Take me back to town. I can't do this."

"Yes, you can."

Old memories rose from the recesses of her mind. "Please, Cam. This is too much."

"Trust me." He grabbed her hand and drove the car through the ornate gate.

She'd noticed that gate at the first memorial service for her parents and the other parents who had died in the crash. It was the only one she'd ever attended. The angel statues on either side of the gate had given her some comfort that day. She'd thought the angels would somehow protect her parents in the afterlife.

Dylan was standing by his vehicle up ahead.

Cam parked his car next to Dylan's. "Grab your purse, Erica."

Her heart was beating so loudly, she was surprised he couldn't hear it. "You weren't kidding. This is where you're taking me."

"Yes, it is. You need to trust us. Do you?"

"I do with so many things," she answered as trembles rolled through her.

He cupped her chin. "I need you to trust me with everything."

"This is hard, Cam."

"I know it is, sweetheart. You haven't been here in many years, but it is necessary."

"Okay," she said, mystified.

Dylan came up and wrapped his arms around her, pressing his lips to hers. "Hey, baby."

She took a deep breath. "What is this about?"

"I can be a bit macabre."

"You're telling me. I don't really want to be here."

"We're headed to row seven," Dylan said.

That wasn't right. "My parents are buried in row five."

"I know. We'll go there afterwards if you want."

"After what?" Her breaths were shallow and her pulse was fast.

"Just trust me."

As they walked through the departed Destonians, she saw familiar surnames. Blue. Stone. Knight. Wolfe. Ryder. All founding families of the town.

"Here we are." Dylan stopped at a headstone.

She read the inscription and felt her heart seize.

Ronald Boyd
Loving teacher and friend
Born November 7, 1964
Died March 30, 2002

"Why did you bring me here?" she snapped.

"Because I know demons. This is your most hideous demon of all. The motherfucker died before you had a chance to confront him. The whole town lifted him up on a pedestal after he died."

Erica took a deep breath, feeling the ancient panic begin to rise inside her. Even though she had her men, her saviors, her rocks, beside her, Ronald Boyd was right there, too. "I don't understand what you're trying to do here, guys."

"It's time for you to face the fucker and release the hell you've suffered for so long." Dylan's tone remained steady but firm.

"How? The man is dead."

"Thank God." Cam grabbed her hand and squeezed. "Get to the point and fast, bro. Can't you see she's shaking?"

She hadn't been aware that she was. Dylan had called Cam and set this up. They'd ambushed her.

Dylan moved closer to her. "Listen carefully to me, my love. With everything that has happened to you, you haven't given up. The whole town knows that you are strong. You won't go down without a fight. This asshole," he pointed to Boyd's grave, "needs to know that, too. You need to know that yourself."

Cam released her hand and kissed her on the cheek. "I think Dylan is right, baby. Why not try?"

Dylan put his arm around her. "Tell Boyd everything. Tell him he's a motherfucker. Tell him how strong you are."

Her heart was racing. This was crazy.

Dylan removed his sunglasses and fixed his stare on her. "Don't hesitate. Feel your pain. Let it out. This asshole deserves to pay for what he did to you."

Here it was, in living color. She was to face her demon head-on and take her power back. Hadn't that been why the pain had never fully gone away? She'd never gotten the closure she so desperately needed.

"Look at the motherfucker lying at peace," Dylan said. "Not one damn thing in the world to worry about. Never mind that he raped a beautiful, innocent young woman."

She stared at the ground where the monster's remains had been put. "You sonofabitch. You did that to me. You ruined my senior year and many years after. I'd lost my parents, and you came with your sickening, lying smile and forced yourself on me." The syllables felt like acid on her tongue. "I was too young to know how to handle that. But I'm not too young now."

Filled with rage, she grabbed her gun out of her purse and fired a shot into Boyd's grave. "That was for betraying me into believing you were my friend, asshole." Another shot. "That was for your slimy grin, bastard." Another shot. "That was for holding me down, you prick." Another shot. "That was for not giving me a choice, you monster." Another shot. "That was for taking away my innocence, you scumbag." She glared at the grave and fired the last shot. "And that was for raping me, motherfucker. I'm not too young now."

She felt all her power return. Her demon was dead. Really dead. No longer would he rise inside her mind to terrify her at night.

She looked at Cam and Dylan, her angels. They'd protected her and taught her how to protect herself. "I just shot a dead man."

Dylan nodded. "You surprised me, baby. You unloaded every bullet into that bastard's cold dead corpse."

Her eyes widened. "Did I just break the law?" She turned to Cam. "Shooting a gun in a cemetery has to be illegal."

Cam shrugged. "So? We're the only ones here. Any witnesses are dead, so they won't be talking."

"Oh my God. What if I had miss and hit the tombstone? One of my shots might've ricocheted and got one of you."

"You didn't miss," Dylan said.

"Once again, you've proven what kind of shot you are, baby," Cam added.

She reached for them, and they wrapped their arms around her.

They are my forever.

"I'd like to go see my parents now."

Chapter Eighteen

7:50 a.m., Friday – TBK Tower, Destiny, Colorado

Erica walked into Matt and Sean's office, realizing that it had been two weeks since she'd been abducted. Not enough time to forget, if there ever would be, but still she felt better being back in her routine.

When they'd left the cemetery Monday night, her men had taken her straight to Sam O'Leary's office. She'd broken down and told him everything, crying as he held her in his arms. It felt so good to let the past go. She still had a lot to work through, but she knew she could do it with Dylan and Cam by her side.

"Hi, Erica. You look like you're feeling better," Sean said, looking up from his screen.

"Can't keep a good woman down for long," she told him. "How's it coming with getting Kip's code out of the system?"

"We're on it. We've isolated most of it, but there are sleepers that we're still searching for," Matt said. "What can we do for you?"

"I'd like my laptop back, if you don't mind."

"I haven't had a chance to check it out. Can I hold onto it through the weekend?" Sean asked. "It might've gotten damaged when those Russians took you."

"I've dropped it before at home. It's indestructible."

"Kind of like you, I bet." Matt opened a drawer and brought out her laptop. "Here you go."

She took it. "Thanks."

"Please let us know if anything weird pops up on your screen,"

Sean advised.

"Weird?"

They both pointed to the white board on the wall.

Matt sighed. "If you see that, call us right away."

She looked at the strange code. *Gen1usKLw1ns.* "What does it mean?"

"It's Kip Lunceford's calling card. So far, whenever we find it buried in the code, it doesn't do anything," Sean told her. "It seems benign, but we're still working through a lot of lines of code to make sure."

"Probably just an egomaniac's way of getting attention," Matt said. "The other parts of his code are much more destructive, but we've taken care of a big chunk of it. Another month, and we'll have TBK's system clean."

"Thanks guys," she said, heading for the door and glancing back at Kip's digital calling card one more time. *Gen1usKLw1ns.* "I'll be sure and call you if that pops up on my screen today."

* * * *

7:57 a.m., Friday – Sheriff's Office, Destiny, Colorado

Dylan shook his head. His gut was twisted into a knot of rage. "This can't be right, Black."

The man had come himself to Destiny to deliver the bad news.

Cam was beside him, as pissed and frustrated as he was. Ethel sat in the chair in front of the desk.

"Sorry, Strange, but it's true." Easton Black, his former boss at the Agency, sat in the other chair. Like him, Black was never without his shades. "As I told your sheriff and judge before, the laptop with the e-mails from Mitrofanov to the president of Spetssetstorsky Construction has vanished."

* * * *

8:02 a.m., Friday – TBK Tower, Destiny, Colorado

Erica sat at her desk and turned on her laptop. Knowing it would take a minute to go through all of the new TBK security protocols before she could get to work, she got up and went to get a cup of coffee from the snack bar.

* * * *

8:02 a.m., Friday – Sheriff's Office, Destiny, Colorado

Cam was enraged by the turn of events. Mitrofanov was about to be released. "How can this be?"

Jason sat behind his desk, his face storming like the rest of them. "I thought the CIA was impenetrable."

"There's no system or place that can't be breached." Black sighed. "The documented proof had been sent to The US Consulate General in Yekaterinburg, Russia. My man on the ground had paperwork that showed Mitrofanov as the corporate secretary of the shill company."

"Then all we need is to get that documentation here to the States. We can keep the bastard locked up," Cam said. "There's ten million dollars of the Knights' money we can try to get back, too."

* * * *

8:03 a.m., Friday – TBK Tower, Destiny, Colorado

Erica looked at her screen and was happy to see her solitaire game pop up. She tapped her laptop. "Maybe you're not as indestructible as everyone believed."

Her head was spinning. She wasn't ready to face the tons of e-mails she knew would be waiting for her. She stared at the screen. *Play Again?*

Why not one game before I dive in? She clicked the button and a prompt appeared. *Password?* There had never been a password to play the game before.

"Damn, this is taking security to the extreme." She stared at the flashing cursor. "Surely this doesn't have anything to do with Kip's viruses in our systems. His calling card didn't pop up."

She sighed, thinking about the strange jumble that was on the Texan's whiteboard.

Her fingers went to the keyboard and without a thought she typed in *Gen1usKLw1ns.*

* * * *

8:04 a.m., Friday – Sheriff's Office, Destiny, Colorado

"Yekaterinburg?" Dylan remembered the agent who had been assigned there, or more like sentenced for a big screw-up. "The man you had there was Grayson. Is he still on that assignment?"

"You've been gone four years. How can you remember that? "

"I haven't forgotten much."

"Grayson is dead, and there is no trace of the documents he had."

* * * *

8:05 a.m., Friday – TBK Tower, Destiny, Colorado

Erica's laptop screen flickered several times. Lines of code that reminded her of the Matrix movie flashed before her eyes.

Kip Lunceford's fingerprints.

She picked up the receiver of her desk phone to call Matt and Sean, but there was static on the line. There had been trouble with all the TBK lines from time to time with the new security protocols in place.

* * * *

8:05 a.m., Friday – Sheriff's Office, Destiny, Colorado

Dylan heard Ethel sigh, and he felt every muscle in his body tighten.

"Jason, you have to let Mitrofanov go." She shook her head. "There's nothing else you have that lets you legally hold him any longer."

Dylan didn't like having to work within the confines of the law in this kind of situation.

There was more discussion between Cam, Black, Jason, and Ethel, but none of it led to a different outcome.

The bastard was going to be released.

Jason went back to Mitrofanov's cell. When he brought the fucker back through his office, the smile on his fat face made Dylan sick.

"Your Honor," Niklaus said, bowing slightly to Ethel. "We've not had the pleasure."

"There's no pleasure from me, Mr. Mitrofanov," she snapped back. "None at all."

"Pity. For a woman of your age, you're quite lovely." Then the creep turned around the room as if he'd conquered all of them. In a way, he had. "I could sue you, Sheriff. I could sue all of you for false arrest."

"Try it," Jason said through clenched teeth. "Make my day."

Why was it that assholes like this mobster got to skate? Unlike Cam, Dylan hated how the wheels of justice ran, especially now. Especially when it came to Erica's safety.

Mitrofanov turned and looked at him and Cam. "You two have quite a job on your hands."

"What do you mean?" he asked flatly, weighing his options.

"I'm just a concerned citizen. I've heard the whispers of what's going on around town." The bastard smiled. "How is Miss Erica? I'm sure you two know how bad things can happen to good people. She's one of the prettiest good girls I've ever seen."

Dylan punched the bastard in the face.

Mitrofanov stumbled and fell to the floor.

Dylan hadn't lost his control. Quite the contrary. He was making a point to the bastard. He wanted Niklaus focused on him not on Erica. *Come for me, fucker. I've been trained on how to deal with your kind.*

"I should sue." Niklaus glared at all of them and rubbed his chin.

Cam looked down at the fat piece of shit. "Why don't you sue me and my brother, asshole?"

Mitrofanov took a deep breath and a smile reappeared on his ugly face. "But I wouldn't dream of it. I'm new here."

When it came to scumbags like Niklaus Mitrofanov, there was only one course of action. For the first time since the incident that made him choose to leave the Agency, Dylan was actually considering taking a human life again. One less mobster above ground would make the world a better place.

Niklaus got back on his feet, bumping into Cam, who stepped back. "This is my home now. Destiny. What a name for a town. My son died here. He was so misguided. I, too, had a past in crime. That was long ago, you understand. A lifetime ago. I just want to get to know everyone here and become a leader in the community. You'll see." Niklaus held out his hand to Dylan. "You, sir, will be the first to mend the fences between us."

"Hell will freeze over before I ever shake your hand," he told the bastard.

* * * *

8:09 a.m., Friday – TBK Tower, Destiny, Colorado

Erica tried her office phone again, but still heard nothing but static. The Texans needed to get that fixed. She reached into her purse for her cell to call them. It vibrated in her hand. She looked at the tiny screen and saw she'd gotten a text from Cam. He must've found his cell.

Meet me by your car in the parking lot. ASAP.

* * * *

8:11 a.m., Friday – Lobby in TBK Tower, Destiny, Colorado

Dylan was first through the door and past security. Cam was right behind. They were rushing to get to Erica. With Mitrofanov back on the streets, he and Cam had to make sure she was safe. She wouldn't like going back to being escorted everywhere, but that was just how it had to be until Niklaus was either back in jail, out of Destiny, or dead.

When the doors opened to the executive floor, there was no sign of Erica anywhere.

Dylan went to her desk and saw a strange code on her screen. Then something he recognized from the day she'd been kidnapped by the Russians filled the screen. *Gen1usKLw1ns*. His heart seized.

"This is Lunceford's code."

"Where could she be?" Cam asked frantically.

"I'm about to find out." Dylan headed to the elevator. When they got inside, he put his password in the keypad. He punched in Erica's employee number, which he'd memorized long ago.

"Erica Coleman left the building from exit three five seconds ago," a digitized voice informed,

"She's in the parking lot," Dylan told him, punching the first floor button on the elevator.

* * * *

8:11 a.m., Friday – TBK's parking lot, Destiny, Colorado

Erica looked around the lot but didn't see Cam. There were only cars and a couple of men smoking to her left.

She reached in her purse to get her cell and saw the pistol that Dylan had bought her.

The hairs on the back of her neck popped up.

The men smoking…I've seen them before.

Where?

The sheriff's office.

They were Mitrofanov's men.

Her heart began thudding like a jackhammer in her chest.

Inside the building was safety. She wouldn't be alone there. *Don't panic.* There could've been a million other reasons the two tatted thugs were here other than to take her and put her in a trunk—*or worse.*

She kept her hand in the purse, but instead of grabbing her cell she clutched her gun. Risking a glance at the two men, she saw one of them was pointing a gun at her. Instantly, her self-defense training kicked in.

Simultaneously, she fired her weapon at the man with the pistol and crouched to the ground behind a car.

Had she hit him? She wasn't sure, but she heard footsteps headed her way and she began crawling the opposite direction.

She thought about screaming for help, but didn't, worrying it might tip the men off on where she was located before anyone could come to her aid. She remained silent through all the violent shakes.

Between two cars, she leaned her back against a tire of one of them and said a silent prayer. *God, don't let me die. Please.* Images of Dylan and Cam came into her mind. With every panicky breath, she wished they were here with her. *As much as I need them, I must focus. I can't be shaking like this.*

Keeping her finger on the trigger of her gun ready in case either of the men found her, Erica heard another shot. *I know they're trying to kill me.* She plastered her body against the car and clenched her jaw. *I don't want to die. Not today. Not without seeing Dylan and Cam.*

"Erica?" *Dylan's voice.*

Had she heard right?

"Sweetheart?" *Cam's voice.*

It has to be them. She heard footsteps coming her way. Her body tensed, still unsure. *God, please let it be them.*

Dylan's tone was anxious. "It's all clear, baby. Where are you?"

It is them. She jumped up and saw her men just a few spaces away. "Over here. I'm over here." She ran into their arms, as tears of relief flooded down her cheeks. "I thought I'd never see you again. I love you."

"I love you, baby." Dylan kissed her.

Cam held her tight. "I love you, sweetheart."

Thankfully, they'd found her.

Although she was still shaking, Erica knew she was safe.

* * * *

9:03 a.m., Friday – TBK's parking lot, Destiny, Colorado

Cam held Erica tight. Dylan stood protectively on the other side of her.

Every employee of TBK was standing behind the crime scene tape that Nicole had put up around the parking lot.

Doc Ryder had pronounced Mitrofanov's henchmen dead on the scene.

"This is an open and shut case of self-defense," Jason said. "But let's go over it one more time, okay?"

"Sure, but it most definitely is self-defense." Dylan grabbed her hand. "Erica shot the asshole who had a gun pointed at her. We came out of TBK Tower and I shot the other one, who was pulling out his pistol as his buddy crashed to the ground."

"If Cam and Dylan hadn't arrived when they did, the other man might've…I don't want to think about that." Erica sighed.

"Baby, we did arrive." Cam brushed the hair out of her eyes. "We're here for you. Always."

"It's a complicated mess, that's for sure," Jason said. "I get that Niklaus must've lifted your cell, Cam, when you were in my office. I'm not sure how we can prove that, but I'm hoping we can. He must've given it to his nephew. The text Erica got was certainly from the dead man. What I don't get is why? Why did they want to lure her out here?"

"Do you think it has something to do with the strange code that showed up on my screen after I typed in Kip's calling card into the password field?" Erica asked.

Matt and Sean came out of the tower. Dylan had sent them to retrieve her laptop for the sheriff right after the shooting.

Sean walked up with it in his hand. "Her abduction wasn't just about the ten million but more about getting Kip's code back into the system via Erica's laptop. The two guys who took her must've been given a flash drive and loaded the code on it after they'd put her in the trunk. They left it for us to find, thinking we would not suspect it had anything to do with her kidnapping. Once it got logged back into TBK's system, Mitrofanov's hacker was back inside."

"We uncovered an automated message that was sent from Erica's laptop after she entered Kip's strange code into the solitaire game," Matt told them.

"Give me that," Jason said, clearly irritated. "That's evidence. You shouldn't have tampered with it."

"No?" Sean said. "Do you know what the differences are between a Trojan, a worm, and a memory resident virus?"

Jason shook his head.

Matt chimed in. "We're your best bet then, Sheriff."

"I'll need to deputize you or at least give you a contract to work for my office then. That'll cross the *t's* and dot the *i's* for me."

"Why not deputize everyone," Nicole said, walking up beside Jason.

"Don't worry. You're my official deputy."

"No. I'm serious, Jason." Nicole pointed to the bodies on the pavement. "As long as Niklaus Mitrofanov and his gang are allowed to walk freely on the streets of Destiny, I say let's deputize the whole town. Everyone is packing anyway."

Sean shook his head as if to clear his thoughts. "The hacker we're still chasing must've been notified that the virus had been activated. That's when he must've reached out to Mitrofanov's organization about the threat of exposure by Erica."

Dylan nodded. "Jason, these two Texans know more about tracking down cyber criminals than anyone else in the country."

"Then I most definitely am going to put a badge on both of them. I still think Kip's involved, but I can't figure out how. That new warden has him locked up tight."

"Yes, but don't forget Niklaus went to see him thanks to one dirty politician," Dylan said.

"Let me through." The distinct Russian accent hit Cam's ears like a razor, and he pulled Erica in even tighter and let his hand find the butt of his gun in case it was needed.

"Speak of the devil," Nicole grumbled.

"Let me get to my nephews." Mitrofanov stepped over the yellow tape, followed by his two sons. He ran to the corpses and dropped to the ground next to them. "Gleb. Gerasim. *Moy milyy plemyannikov. Chto oni sdelali dlya vas.*"

Cam had no idea what the Russian words meant, but it was clearly about the two stiffs and the rage their fat uncle was feeling.

Niklaus turned his angry glare to Jason. "You will pay, Sheriff. These boys were innocent."

"Not true, Mitrofanov. TBK's cameras captured everything. If you want to see the footage, I'm sure we can arrange a viewing. Now, if you don't want me to arrest you, leave. This is a crime scene. You can collect the bodies of your nephews after the autopsies are finished by Doc Ryder and not before."

"Papa, let's go," one of his sons said, bending down and pulling him up to his feet.

Niklaus closed his eyes. When they opened, the slimeball's demeanor was completely changed. "Please forgive my outburst, Sheriff. The loss of two young lives is hard for an old man. I had no idea my troubled nephews had slipped so far. I only wanted the best for them."

"Nice story, Mitrofanov," Cam said. "Jason will connect this whole shit to you and then you'll be going to prison where you belong."

"And if he can't?"

"Don't try to goad me," he said, feeling the rage bubble up inside him. "I'm not that stupid."

"No. I suppose you're not." Niklaus shook his head. "A sad day for all of Destiny."

Then the fat fuck walked back the way he'd come.

"The bastard means to stay in town it seems to me," Nicole said.

"He has to until we get this case fully investigated," Jason said. "Fuck, I don't want him in my town."

"None of us do, Jason," Dylan said.

No truer words had ever been spoken.

"May I go, Jason?" Erica asked. "I really need a drink of water."

The sheriff nodded. "Of course. I might have more questions for you later. I'll call you if I do."

"Thank you."

Cam put his arm around the bravest woman he'd ever known, his and Dylan's woman. "Let's get you out of here, baby."

Chapter Nineteen

Dylan pulled into Erica's driveway. Things seemed to be settling down after the shootout in TBK's parking lot a week ago. Jason hadn't been able to pin any of it on Mitrofanov, so the mobster was free to go. Even though Niklaus still owned the house on MacDavish, he hadn't come back to town since he'd left to bury his nephews in Chicago. Everyone, especially Jason, hoped the mobster wouldn't come back. Ever.

Erica was doing better each day. She'd been meeting with Sam during her lunch hour. She was learning to accept the past without regret.

Expecting to find Erica, Dylan walked into her house and found Cam, who was standing in the middle of the living room holding a piece of paper. "Where's Erica? I thought you were supposed to meet us at Phong's."

Cam frowned. "And I thought *you* were supposed to meet *us* at Phongs. Check out the note she left us." His brother handed the paper over. "Apparently, our girl is playing tricks on both of us."

He took the note and couldn't help but smile at the message she'd left them.

Guys,

I love you so much. You saved me in so many ways. What you did for me at the cemetery helped me reach closure. No woman could be happier than I am. You're the reason. I know you said that we needed to go slow on the BDSM, but I'm ready. Really ready. I've got a private room for us at Phase Four. I'm not ready for any of the public stages, but I am ready to be the woman you deserve in every way. More than that, I can't wait to be that woman.

Waiting for you in room 7.

With all my love,

Your submissive,

erica

"What do you think?" Cam asked.

"I liked that she spelled her name with a little *e* and not a capital letter. Nice and submissive." Dylan chuckled, feeling his cock become uncomfortable in his pants. "I think this is the worst case of topping from the bottom I've ever seen in my life."

"I know, but do you think she's right?" Cam's tone had an obvious heat to it. Erica's note had impacted Cam the same way it had him. "Is she ready?"

"There's only one way to find out. If our little sub wants to play, I'm going to give her my best. I need to stop at my place and change clothes and get some things."

"Me, too," Cam said. "Should I bring the TENS unit?"

"Bring everything. I am." Dylan put his arm around his brother. "We need to bring our A-game for Erica. God, I'm proud of her."

Erica might've started the ball rolling tonight, but he and Cam would be the ones in control from now on. He couldn't wait to see her lips shivering in pleasure-filled delight.

"Same here." Cam smiled. "She's going to do great."

"Yes, she will," he said, heading out the door to the woman he loved and shared with the man who was his best friend and brother.

* * * *

The temperature was perfect in room seven of Phase Four, but Erica sat on the wooden bench shivering. There were all kinds of contraptions in the space, and all of them wicked looking.

Mr. Gold had agreed to let her in, though she had let her membership lapse, but only after Amber, Megan, and Nicole had cornered him. She loved those women.

She slipped off the bench and paced around the fifteen by fifteen square space. The door was locked. Mr. Gold said he would give the key to Dylan and Cam when they arrived, but no one else. She wore a black bikini top, leather mini, fishnet stockings, and red pumps. The raincoat she'd walked into the club with had covered her. Nicole had pointed out that it also made her look like a female flasher, which made Amber and Megan laugh.

Erica had chuckled herself at the comment. She wasn't quite ready to be public with her play, but she was definitely ready to play with Cam and Dylan. She was theirs in every way.

She considered taking off her clothes before her guys arrived, but didn't think they would like finding her naked. So, she didn't.

She went to the door and checked the deadbolt again. Still locked. What time was it? They had to have gotten the note at least thirty minutes ago. What was taking them so long? Then she had a horrible thought. What if they weren't coming? What if something had come up at TBK that demanded their attention and they couldn't make it? Her guys certainly would've called or texted her, wouldn't they? Cam would've for sure. Had Dylan's old demons surfaced again? What if…?

Erica knew she was just being silly. They'd proven their love to her again and again. Whatever was keeping them wasn't going to keep them away for long. She just had to be patient. But she wasn't patient. Not even a little.

She took a deep breath, trying to calm her excitement and nervousness. The moment she'd written the note, her anticipation tingles had begun. Walking into the club, they'd gotten warm. When she'd closed the door and locked herself into room seven, they'd gotten hotter. After she took off her raincoat, they'd become violently molten.

A knock on the door had her heart jumping up in her throat. "Mr. Gold?"

Another knock had her grabbing for her raincoat.

Erica's self-defense lessons kicked in and she crouched to the side of the door. No weapons were allowed in Phase Four, so she didn't have the pink-handled gun that Dylan had given her. She did have pepper spray in the pocket of her raincoat.

Another knock. This one was louder, harder, more urgent.

"This room is taken," she said loudly, hoping it was just some lost member of the club.

The deadbolt unlocked.

Her pulse raced in her veins and she crouched down, bracing for the worst.

The door swung open.

Dylan walked in. "We know this room is taken, sub."

He carried a black satchel, but it wasn't what he was carrying that had gooseflesh popping up on her skin. It was what he was wearing. From the waist up, he wore only his sunglasses. He had on dark jeans that were held up by a wide leather belt. Even his black boots made him look intimidating and delicious.

Cam came in behind him, carrying his own satchel. His Dom gear was different than Dylan's. He wore only black leathers—vest, pants, a strap around each muscled bicep and military boots. If danger had a first name, it would be Cameron Strange.

Dylan knelt down in front of her and cupped her chin. Then he turned to Cam. "Look at this sub crouching on the ground. Have you ever seen such a pretty sight?" Dylan straightened up. "Stand on your feet, sweetheart."

With her heart picking up speed, Erica obeyed.

"Cam and I are in control, not you. You understand that?" His tone stung her.

She lowered her eyes. "I do."

"We do not tolerate lies."

Nodding, she looked down at her feet.

"Look at me, sub." She felt him cup her chin, nudging her to look at him.

She swallowed hard and got to her feet. "Yes, Sir."

Dylan straightened up, which had him towering over her again. "It's Master."

"Yes, Master."

"I like the sound of that." Cam smiled, making his face look even sexier. "You've been a very naughty girl, sub."

She wasn't sure if he was teasing or serious. "What did I do, Masters?"

Dylan sat on a bench and patted the spot beside him. "Come sit by me."

She instantly obeyed, trembling from the masculine energy her men were sending throughout the room and into her.

Cam began unloading the sex toys from his satchel, placing them on the tables around the room.

Dylan caressed her cheek. His fingers were sending ripples of heat through her body. She stared at her own reflection in his sunglasses, and saw how flushed her cheeks were.

"Let me start by talking about your little game of deception." Dylan's tone was a mixture of kindness and strength. "You lied to both me and Cam about who was going to be at Phong's and who was to pick you up."

"B–But it was only to get you two together to see my note at the same time. That was all I was trying to do," she said.

Cam looked at her, eyebrows raised in question.

"Master," she added, her voice shaking.

"Didn't Cam and I tell you that we would know when you were ready for BDSM or not? We were very clear that we would be the ones to take you to the club, correct?"

"Yes, Sir."

"Your impatience got the better of you. That's why you concocted this devious plan to get what you wanted."

"But I am ready." What they'd done for her at Boyd's grave had killed her demons for good. She was ready to dive headfirst into the life.

"There you go with your 'buts' again." Dylan placed his hands on both her shoulders. He leaned his head against hers until her eyelashes were touching the lenses of his sunglasses. "The only way to break you of that bad habit is to warm up that pretty butt of yours. Warm it up really nice until it's a bright pink. You've been bad sub. You must be punished, understand?"

Her belly flip-flopped. "Yes, Master."

"Did you eat before you came here tonight?" Cam asked, sitting down beside her opposite Dylan.

"Yes, Master."

"Good." He stroked her cheek, and his gaze made her warm. "You're going to need your strength for what we've got in store for you."

Her lips trembled. "I'm sorry," she told them. "I just wanted to show you I was ready for this, to be the best sub I can be."

"Sweetheart, you already have," Cam said as Dylan began unloading his implements of pleasure around the room. "We know you've had some training in the life, but it's been a year or more since you've visited the club, right?"

"Yes, Sir."

"Dylan and I are going to reintroduce you to the life in ways I doubt you've ever experienced in your previous training." He sounded so confident and in control. "We're going to start you on the St. Andrew's Cross. Have you ever been on one before?"

She shook her head. "I know what it is. It's the giant 'X' thing. I've been on a spanking bench a few times."

Dylan laughed, pulling the St. Andrew's Cross to the center of the room. "Listen to our sub, Cam. She's so fucking cute." He turned to her. "Baby, you're going to be on all kinds of things, but your final destination is going to be under me. Got it? My cock is going to feel that tight bare pussy of yours squeezing my seed out."

She gulped as dizzy heat rolled through her at his lusty talk.

Cam removed her top, releasing her breasts. He pinched her nipples, making her breath catch in her chest. Then he pulled her mini down and removed it.

Cam's hot gaze zeroed in on her pussy. "No panties? Very nice."

She'd expected going natural would entice them, and she'd been right.

He and Dylan guided her to the contraption, face-first, leaving her backside exposed completely for their pleasure. She could feel their hands on her, pushing her forward until every part of her front was pressing against the boards. Her cells fired hot inside her, and her pussy began to dampen. They put cuffs on her wrists and attached them to the top parts of the *X*, creating a *Y* shape out of her body. They bent down and forced her legs apart, also placing cuffs on each ankle and attaching them to the bottom of the cross. She was splayed out for them. Standing in this fashion wasn't uncomfortable but it was unfamiliar.

She was glad when she didn't show any signs of panicking. She was being restrained and she was okay with it. Her quick breaths and racing heart was from excitement not fear.

"Time for a quick run-through of your safe words, baby." Dylan's voice took on a professorial tone, as if she was taking some kind of class or lecture from him. In a way, she was. "Red. Yellow. Green."

"Yes, Master. The colors."

"Good. And what state is my little sub in now?" he asked firmly.

"Green," she whispered, feeling expectant tingles rush through her.

She vowed to herself to make them proud, to show them she was more than ready to endure whatever it was they meant to do to her. "Red" was her ultimate safe word, but it would not be needed tonight. She was ready to surrender herself to them fully.

Cam came around the cross and gazed at her with his sexy eyes. "You lied to us. Not good, sweetheart."

"She must be punished for that," Dylan said from behind her.

She gulped, feeling so tiny and feminine under his hot stare. "Yes, Master."

Cam cupped her chin. "Brace yourself. I'm going to blindfold you."

"I'm ready, Sir," she said proudly, steeling her will against any doubt or anxiety. What happened at Lover's Beach would not happen tonight or ever again. Cam winked at her and then placed a blindfold over her eyes.

"Color?" he asked.

"Green, Master."

She listened to the tap of their boots on the floor as they walked around her.

"Look at our sub," Cam said. "She's the sexiest thing I've ever laid eyes on."

"Yes, she is. This ass," Dylan's hands cupped her bottom, "is going to look even prettier in a bright shade of pink." She felt his hand glide up and down her back, and shivers popped up everywhere on her body.

Being spread out for them this way made her heartbeats thud rapidly until sweat layered her skin. Without sight, the only images that appeared in her mind were of them in their sexy Dom gear, causing lines of heat to rip through her, settling between her thighs until her clit began to throb like mad.

"We're going to begin with Cam's TENS unit, baby," Dylan informed. "Do you know what that is?"

"No, Master," she confessed.

"This little sub hasn't had much training at all," Dylan teased, his tone deep and lusty. "That's just how I hoped she would be. Training her in the life is going to be such a fucking pleasure."

"Hold your horses, cowboy," Cam said with a laugh. "One thing at a time. Sweetheart, a TENS unit was developed for pain management but has been used in BDSM for some time for play. TENS stands for 'transcutaneous electrical nerve stimulation' and is used by doctors for therapy for patients suffering from chronic pain."

"You sound too clinical, bro." Dylan stroked her hair. "You're going to love it, baby. We're going to place its electrodes in your pussy and your ass."

She couldn't imagine what having a literal charge of electricity on her most sensitive flesh would do to her.

"Time to get you nice and stretched out for this." Someone, Cam she suspected, fingered her pussy, and she got even wetter.

One of her men applied lubricant to her anus, making her dizzy with desire.

Soon, she was writhing in her restraints.

"Time for you to feel the bite of my TENS," Cam said, stretching her pussy lips and placing what she knew must be the little electrodes within her body. "What color?"

She took a deep breath and paused. "Green."

She heard a click, and instantly a hot jolt shot through her vagina. Her pussy clenched tight, and her entire body began to shiver.

She heard another click and felt the electricity vanish and her pussy soften.

"Very good, sweetheart." Dylan's praise made her tingle like mad. "Can you take more?"

She nodded, chewing on her lower lip.

Another click. The jolt zipped into her womb, causing lines of heat to shoot through her body. Her nipples were budding, her pussy was dampening, her clit was throbbing. The pressure rose inside her and her need expanded beyond what she'd ever experienced before.

Click.

The current vanished and she felt her body loosen up. The TENS was ramping up her want, which was already crushing and overwhelming.

Click.

The voltage penetrated every one of her nerve endings, causing fiery sensations inside her body.

Click.

Though the circuit was broken, her urgency was not. Instead it seemed to be compounding with every switch on and off of the TENS.

She felt one of her men remove the TENS unit's connectors from her pussy. A flood of uncontrollable trembles rocked through her. As the electrodes were placed inside her ass, she felt the pressure augment and expand within her.

"Let's up the power on our sub," he told Cam. "She can take it."

"I think you're right."

"Ready?" Dylan asked.

"Yes, Master."

Click.

The shock was stronger, though only a little, and caused her fingers and toes to curl.

Click.

During the "off" moment of the TENS, she felt liquid slipping down her thighs and knew she was getting even more soaked with each jolt.

Click. On.

More need. More want.

Click. Off.

She felt lips brush over her ass as fingers moved to her pussy and clit, teasing her into a total state of abandon and thirst.

"I can't wait to taste this delicious cream of yours, baby, but we have to spank you," Dylan said. "You were a very naughty sub coming here unescorted by us."

"I was bad, Master. Very bad," she teased, needing his touch so terribly, even if that came from his open hand slapping against her ass.

"There she goes again, Cam," Dylan said. "Trying to top us from the bottom."

"I heard. We've got quite a job in front of us training our sub."

"Yes, we do."

A hand came down on her ass with two sharp whacks.

"Those are to remind you who is in charge of your pleasure. Understand?" Dylan asked.

Her body was vibrating with desire. "Yes, Master."

Whack. Whack. Whack.

Every time the palm of his hand connected to her bottom, she felt warmth dripping from her pussy. Her clit was burning and her nipples were aching.

"Your turn, bro," Dylan said to Cam.

"Yes, it is." Cam's lips feathered against her ear. "You will not lie to us again."

Whack. Whack. Whack.

As his slaps to her ass continued to rain down on her flesh, She never felt so exposed, open, and in a state of dizzy submission.

"You are mine, baby. I'm in charge of your pleasure. I will make you feel things you never thought possible."

Whack.

Tears pricked at her eyes, but she held them back. Her ass burned from his and Dylan's spanking. Lines of heat spread everywhere in her body, but seemed to swirl even hotter in her pussy.

"Surrendering to Dylan and me will allow you to just feel. It will get you out of your doubt and fears. You'll see."

His dominance thrilled her. "Yes, Master."

Before all that had happened the last several months, she'd thought her life was as good as it was going to get. Not great, but not horrible either. Then all the crazy stuff with the Russians had happened. She'd never expected that terrible event to lead her into the arms of the two men she loved with all her heart and would spend the rest of her life with.

Dylan removed her blindfold. She blinked several times, bringing him into focus.

"You did good, baby. But we're not done yet."

"Yes, Master." It was funny how calling him and Cam that in this room seemed so right. She realized that was what BDSM was about, bringing lovers closer in trust. This was play, their play. They could do anything they desired as long as they were together. If they pushed too hard, she could stop it with a word. Not hard enough…well, she could…what had Dylan called it? Topping from the bottom. She could do that. Being naughty sometimes would be fun, especially if it ended at Phase Four in a room like this one. She belonged here with them.

"I want to feel your pretty lips on my cock," Dylan told her as Cam removed her restraints from the St. Andrew's Cross. "Would you like to taste my dick, baby?"

"Yes, Master," she confessed eagerly. More than anything, she wanted to please him and Cam.

When they helped her off the cross, she saw they were completely nude now. They must've stripped while she'd been blindfolded. Their ten-inch cocks were rock hard and pointing to the ceiling.

Cam placed a folded towel in front of her on the concrete floor. "On your knees," he commanded.

She obeyed. The cotton softened the feel of the hard surface, but only a little.

"Lower your gaze, sub. Be respectful," Dylan ordered.

Again, she complied with their demands. *I am theirs. They love me and I love them. I want to make them proud.*

"Hands behind your back," Cam told her.

When she did, he placed handcuffs on her. The icy steel on her wrists sent several quakes through her body.

Cam moved back in front of her next to Dylan. With her eyes down, all she could see were their feet. They'd clearly positioned her this way to reinforce their dominance over her. It was working. She felt completely subdued. All she wanted to do was whatever would make them proud of her.

"Time for a taste of those lips," Dylan said. She felt his fingers on her cheek. "Look at me, baby."

She tilted her head up and he bent down and devoured her mouth. With her hands behind her back in the cuffs, there was nothing she could do but surrender to his overwhelming kiss that only added to the tormenting pressure inside her.

When Dylan released her mouth, Cam's lips took residence on hers, lingering there with unspoken demands of unconditional surrender. Submitting to them felt so right, so necessary. They would care for her. They would keep her safe. They would love her until the end of their days, and she would do the same with all her heart.

Cam moved his kiss to her neck. His warm breath caressed her ear, sending hot trembles up and down her spine. "I want to make love to your gorgeous mouth," he whispered. "Would you like that, sub?"

"Yes, Master."

"You will suck my dick and Dylan's dick. Understand?"

She nodded.

He straightened up, positioning the head of his cock right next to her lips. It was awkward to not have the use of her hands for the task, but it wasn't impossible. She leaned forward and licked the tip of his dick, finding a slick pearly reward from him on the slit. Her want was rising tenfold as her lips traced up and down his shaft. The deep groan that came from Cam's muscled chest made her even hotter. She swallowed his dick, sucking on him with all her might. She felt his hands on the back of her head, urging her on. Sucking as hard as she could, she created a vacuum of her mouth. When his cock hit the back of her throat, she felt completely his. Her whole body shook from the intense desire racing through her. Dylan knelt down beside her and slid his fingers over her pussy, causing her to moan.

"That's my baby," Cam growled hungrily. "Vibrate your throat on my cock."

"Make him come, sub," Dylan commanded. "Swallow all of him." He pressed his thumb on her clit, and the pressure inside her rose higher and higher.

She sucked on Cam, bobbing up and down his dick, swirling her tongue with every pass.

"Fuck. That feels so good." His breaths were labored.

Her heart was racing. She was greedy for his essence, so she tightened her lips even more around his cock. Dylan moved behind her and took her handcuffs off. He rubbed her wrists and guided one hand to his cock and the other to Cam's. As she began stroking Dylan's cock, she felt Cam's dick jerk in her throat.

"Coming," he growled.

She felt his seed hit the back of her throat. She drank every drop, relishing in the intimacy they had.

Dylan stepped in front of her. "Suck me, now," he ordered.

She took her lips off Cam and moved to Dylan's cock, swallowing him immediately. His hands tugged on her hair, creating a new round of shivers and need inside her. Up and down, she took him, and her own desire continued ramping up more and more. Soon, she felt his fingers on the back of her head, forcing her to take a little more of him.

"Fuck," he yelled and sent his hot liquid into her mouth.

She looked up at them, proud of her accomplishment.

"You are mine," Dylan said, taking off his sunglasses.

"And mine," Cam added, stroking her hair.

"Yes, Masters."

They helped her to her feet and bent down, each rubbing one of her legs, which had gotten a little numb in the kneeling position that they'd placed her in. God, they could be so sweet and loving.

Dylan lifted her up in his arms. "You've earned your reward, baby."

"I have?"

"Yes, you have."

Out of the corner of her eye she saw Cam stretch out a blanket on the floor. It was white and looked soft and fluffy. Dylan lowered her down to the fabric. He crawled on top of her and kissed her again until the pressure inside her was nearly unbearable. As he moved down her body, tracing his lips the whole way, fire raced along her skin.

Dylan lifted her legs over his shoulder and she brought her feet together, locking them by the ankles. She could feel his stubble on the inside of her thighs. His tormenting tongue circled her pussy, paying extreme attention to her clit. Dylan rolled onto his side, pulling her with him without removing his mouth from her sex. She felt Cam move behind her. Where Dylan's body ran the same direction hers did, though deliciously lower, Cam's was opposite hers. When she felt Cam's tongue on her ass, she moaned as the pressure finally found an escape.

Their mouths sent her into a state of utter euphoria. She clawed at Dylan's head as sensations rocked her entire body. "God, yes. Oh. Yes. Oh."

Dylan moved up her body and sent his cock into her pussy. Cam flipped around and pierced her ass with his dick. Her men had filled her body and stolen her heart.

Their thrusts took her even higher until she couldn't breathe.

She had no idea how long they made love to her this way, but before she knew it she came again and so did Cam and Dylan.

They're mine and I'm theirs.

Chapter Twenty

Erica couldn't eat another bite of the delicious meal. She looked up in the sky at the stars above her brothers' cabin. The night was perfect.

She was still a little sore from the night before at Phase Four. She couldn't wait to go back.

"I hope you left room for dessert," Nicole said. "Apple pie. Of course it's from Blue's, since we still don't have an oven here."

Reed leaned over and kissed her. "When our house is done, we'll have the best appliances money can buy."

"Don't you mean credit can get?" Sawyer laughed. "Don't worry, baby, we'll give you whatever your heart desires."

"You've outdone yourself, Cam," Nicole said. "Our guests at the reception are going to love your steaks."

"Thanks, but I've never grilled for three hundred before."

"I'll help," Dylan said.

"You can't even boil water, bro."

"But I sure can make a mean piece of toast."

Everyone laughed.

Erica looked at Cam and Dylan, glad that they were so relaxed. "Let's help clean up the dishes," she said. "It's late and we probably should be getting back to town soon."

"Not before we play charades," Nicole said with a giggle.

"Charades? Sawyer and Reed hate games, except the ones where money is involved. I doubt that Cam and Dylan would go for that either."

"You're wrong, sweetheart," Dylan said.

"Yes, you are wrong, baby." Cam smiled. "I would love to play a game of charades. Strange team against the Coleman team."

Shocked, she shrugged.

"I've already got the slips of paper made up," Nicole said, pulling out a glass bowl filled with white strips from under her chair.

"I had no idea you liked games so much," she told her. "I'm taking back your wedding gift and getting you some board games. Would you like that better?"

"Depends on what you're taking back," Nicole said with a wink. "My rules are a little different than traditional charades. It's two on one. Two giving the clues and one guessing. Okay?"

"You've really given this some thought, haven't you?" Erica smiled. Nicole brought so much joy wherever she was. "It's okay with me if everyone else is okay with it."

All the men were nodding.

"Let's play," she said, getting into the spirit of the night.

"We'll see who is boss around here," Cam said, standing.

"That's for sure," Dylan added. "Cam and I will give the clues."

"That's good," she told him. "I'm really a good guesser."

Cam reached into the bowl and pulled out a slip. She leaned forward, feeling competitive. Time to show her big brothers who the real winner was. Cam handed the paper over to Dylan. The strangest thing happened next. Dylan took off his sunglasses and placed them on the table, and both her men knelt down in front of her.

"*Three Men and a Baby. Romeo and Juliet. The Little Mermaid.*"

"*The Little Mermaid?*" Dylan mocked.

"*When Harry Met Sally.*"

What else could it be? "Do something else. Please," she said impatiently.

Dylan smiled, his dark eyes brighter than she'd ever seen them before. He reached into the pocket of his jacket and pulled out a ring box. Cam opened it and she gazed at the diamond ring inside.

"*Indecent Proposal.*" She laughed. "I didn't think

props…were…allowed." Then she realized this whole thing was just a ruse. This wasn't a game. Cam and Dylan were actually proposing. "Yes. Yes. Yes."

They each grabbed one of her hands.

Cam's blue gaze made her tingly from head to toe. "We asked your brothers for your hand and they gave us their permission."

"You did?" One thing about Destiny men, they believed in protocols.

"Yes, we did, sweetheart." Dylan squeezed her hand. "The game was Nicole's idea. Now, let's get serious. I love you. I will always love you. Will you make me the happiest man alive? Will you marry me, Erica Coleman?"

"Yes, Dylan Strange. I will marry you."

"I love you, baby. God, you are life itself to me. I want to spend the rest of my life loving you." Cam squeezed her other hand. "Will you marry me, sweetheart?"

"Of course. Yes.

Together, her men put the ring on her finger. Cam and Dylan wrapped her up in their arms, kissing her.

Her brothers came up and kissed her on the cheek, and then slapped Cam and Dylan on their backs.

Nicole gave her a hug. "I'm so happy for you."

"I'm engaged."

"Not for long," Reed said with a chuckle.

"What do you mean by that?" she asked.

Nicole smiled. "We all met yesterday afternoon to plan for tonight."

"Five conspirators, all of you," she said, looking at her ring again. It was white gold with beautiful sparkling round diamonds that surrounded the largest stone, which was an emerald-cut diamond. "This is the most beautiful ring I've ever seen. It's perfect."

"Hey, mine is the most beautiful and you know it, Erica," Nicole teased.

They both laughed.

"So what did you mean when you said I wasn't going to be engaged for long?" she asked Reed. "Are they going to break up with me already or are you just pulling my leg?"

"You better ask them," her brother answered.

"Want to get married next Friday?" Cam and Dylan said together, clearly having rehearsed it.

"Next Friday is my brothers and Nicole's wedding. That's her day."

Nicole stepped in front of her. "Erica, I have no family but these two cowboys and you. You're the sister I never had. I would love to share that day with you. It would be the best wedding gift you could give me."

Erica hugged her. "You're the same for me. I grew up around eight boys. Having you as a sister is a dream come true, but Nicole, planning a wedding is a big deal."

"Yes, it is. You've been helping me with it for the last month. Right? You helped pick the colors, the venue, the minister, the music, everything. Isn't it the kind of wedding you want for yourself?"

"Yes, but—"

"Nicole, Erica always has a but," Dylan interrupted. "You have to be careful with her."

"I've got this, James Bond." Nicole smiled at her. "Please."

"What about a dress?"

"When we were shopping for my dress, I saw how your eyes lit up on that pretty little chiffon with the single strap. It would be perfect for your figure. I've already set up a fitting for you in the morning."

"You were that sure I would say 'yes'?"

"I believe in being prepared. It's part of my law enforcement training."

"You've all made me so happy"—she turned to Cam and Dylan—"especially you two. It sounds so wonderful. Why not have a double wedding. This is Destiny. Unusual things are appreciated and expected."

Cam and Dylan encircled her, kissing her again.

* * * *

Dylan stood with the three other grooms by The Red Dragon statue.

The ceremony was about to get underway in the center of Destiny's park, which had been transformed into a fairy-tale land by Erica and Nicole with the help of the real movers and shakers of Destiny, *the women*. Erica had even wrapped wide colorful ribbons around all four of the dragon statues in the corners of the park. Central Park had never been better.

He looked at all the people who had come to celebrate this day with them. Friends and relatives were smiling, sharing the pleasure of two new young families about to be created. There were over three hundred people in attendance. Alice Blue and her husbands had taken over the job of grilling the steaks for the reception, freeing Cam up for his duties today.

The Knights were on the second row with Megan in between them. They were smiling from ear to ear. They would be celebrating their own wedding in just a week. Jason and his two brothers, Mitchell and Lucas, sat near the back. All three were staring in Phoebe Blue's direction. She sat with her two brothers, Shane and Corey, two men who couldn't be more opposite even if they tried. In front of the Blues were the Stone brothers and Amber. They were already expecting their first child. Dylan couldn't wait to have children with Erica. She was going to be a wonderful mother. Amber's sister Belle sat next to Juan, the kid who had been rescued by both women. The boys' ranch the Stones and the two ladies were setting up was expected to open by Christmas. Shane kept leaning forward and talking to Belle. Corey sat back, but his eyes never left the woman. It sure seemed liked something might be brewing between those three. *God, I've really gone soft. I sound like a hopeless romantic.* What man wouldn't in his situation? He'd found the love of his life and was about to make her his wife.

Ethel O'Leary, who was officiating the ceremony, walked up to them. "Gentlemen, we're ready to begin. If you'll follow me, please."

She led them to the center of the park, meant for the wedding party. Every cut flower in Swanson County must've been there, making a floral wall behind them. They took their places—he and Cam on one side and Sawyer and Reed on the other, with Ethel in between them.

The Destiny Chamber Musicians—Gretchen Hollingsworth on the flute, Patrick O'Leary on the violin, and Norman Little, Lucy's husband, on the upright bass—fired up the wedding march. The crowd stood and turned their attention to the tent that had been set up for the two brides.

Erica and Nicole came out, but all he could see was Erica. She was like an angel, his angel. Her hair was up. She held a bouquet of white roses. He couldn't stop staring at her. He'd worn his sunglasses, today, but he didn't want even a lens to impede his eyes of the vision coming down the aisle, so he took them off. His heart thudded in his chest. He put his arm around Cam, uncaring if it was appropriate or not for the ceremony.

"Erica is ours."

"Yes, she is," his brother and best friend answered. "Now and forever."

Chapter Twenty-One

Dylan listened intently at the door of the warehouse in Odessa, Texas.

He was here with the Texans, who had finally tracked down TBK's hacker, who was inside the building.

It felt good to be running an operation with his old CIA buds again. Really good.

Dylan was always careful during this kind of mission, but now that he was a married man with a wife he adored, he wanted to be especially careful.

Matt and Sean believed the hacker was working for someone else, and so did he. The Russians? Even Kip Lunceford? A corporate competitor of TBK? None of them were sure.

Though only one car, a white 2004 Ford Taurus, was parked outside the warehouse, the hacker might not be alone.

Sean went around back to the only other exit out of the building.

They waited thirty seconds and got Sean's signal that he was in position.

They were about to take out the mastermind who had been eluding them for months. Dylan kicked in the door and rushed in.

Sean came in the back, his gun in his hand and his eyes wide.

The space was filled with the latest and greatest computer equipment, just like the other buildings they had discovered when looking for Erica after her abduction. The difference today was the hacker was here.

"I never expected you to be a woman," Matt said.

"Might be sexist, but me either," Sean added.

The girl's hands were in the air. "I never expected you to find me."

THE END

WWW.CHLOELANG.COM

ABOUT THE AUTHOR

Chloe Lang began devouring romance novels during summers between college semesters as a respite to the rigors of her studies. Soon, her lifelong addiction was born, and to this day, she typically reads three or four books every week.

For years, the very shy Chloe tried her hand at writing romance stories, but shared them with no one. After many months of prodding by an author friend, Sophie Oak, she finally relented and let Sophie read one. As the prodding turned to gentle shoves, Chloe ultimately did submit something to Siren-BookStrand. The thrill of a life happened for her when she got the word that her book would be published.

For all titles by Chloe Lang, please visit
www.bookstrand.com/chloe-lang

Siren Publishing, Inc.
www.SirenPublishing.com

CPSIA information can be obtained at www.ICGtesting.com
Printed in the USA
LVOW10s2107101214

418177LV00022B/1100/P